THE JUNGLE
TEMPLE ORACLE

Books by Mark Cheverton

The Gameknight999 Series
Invasion of the Overworld
Battle for the Nether
Confronting the Dragon

The Mystery of Herobrine Series: A Gameknight999
Adventure
Trouble in Zombie-town
The Jungle Temple Oracle
Last Stand on the Ocean Shore

The Herobrine Reborn Series: A Gameknight999
Adventure
Saving Crafter (Coming soon!)
The Destruction of the Overworld (Coming soon!)
Gameknight999 vs. Herobrine (Coming soon!)

The Algae Voices of Azule Series
Algae Voices of Azule
Finding Home
Finding the Lost

AN UNOFFICIAL NOVEL

THE JUNGLE TEMPLE ORACLE

THE MYSTERY OF HEROBRINE
BOOK TWO
<<< A GAMEKNIGHT999 ADVENTURE >>>

AN UNOFFICIAL MINECRAFTER'S ADVENTURE

MARK CHEVERTON

SKY PONY PRESS
NEW YORK

Copyright ©2015 by Mark Cheverton
First box set edition 2015.

Minecraft® is a registered trademark of Notch Development AB

The Minecraft game is copyright © Mojang AB

Sky Pony Press books may be purchased in bulk at special discounts for sales promotion, corporate gifts, fund-raising, or educational purposes. Special editions can also be created to specifications. For details, contact the Special Sales Department, Sky Pony Press, 307 West 36th Street, 11th Floor, New York, NY 10018 or info@ skyhorsepublishing.com.

Sky Pony® is a registered trademark of Skyhorse Publishing, Inc.®, a Delaware corporation.

Visit our website at www.skyponypress.com.

10 9 8 7 6 5 4 3 2 1

Library of Congress Cataloging-in-Publication Data is available on file.

Cover design by Owen Corrigan
Cover artwork by JiaSen (jiasen.deviantart.com)
Technical consultant - Gameknight999

Box set ISBN: 978-1-63450-210-8
Ebook ISBN: 978-1-63450-097-5

Printed in China

ACKNOWLEDGEMENTS

I'd like to thank my family for their continued support and understanding for my constant, compulsive need to write at 4 a.m. and at night and every minute over the weekends. Without your support, I could have never written these books.

I'd also like to thank Sara Klock for her continual excitement and support from day one of this adventure. Her enthusiasm and energy was contagious and appreciated.

I'd also like to thank the fantastic people at Skyhorse Publishing. Their tireless work is inspiring and keeps me writing when I'm exhausted.

Lastly, thank you to all the readers out there. Your adoption of Gameknight999, Monet113, Crafter, Hunter, and Stitcher into your hearts and imaginations is sincerely appreciated. Keep reading, for there are more adventures coming . . . and watch out for creepers.

WHAT IS MINECRAFT?

Minecraft is an incredibly creative game that can be played either online with people from all over the world, or just played with friends, or played alone. It's likely one of the most creative things I've seen come to computer gaming in a long time. Referred to as a sandbox game, it gives the player the ability to build anything their minds can imagine using textured cubes as their building materials. Of course, most players first build a castle . . . that seems like a rite of passage in Minecraft. Players quickly realize, though, that the rules of physics don't apply to this digital landscape. In Creative mode, you can build floating cities in the sky, a bridge to nowhere, or an underwater village of glass (that was one of the things that were destroyed on my son's server!). I've seen people build massive, ornately decorated spiral staircases that extended from deep down at the bedrock level all the way up to the build limit (layer 255) and others building massive space stations that float in the sky and span hundreds of blocks in all directions. Anything is possible as long as you follow two important rules: 1—everything is made of blocks, and 2—you can build anything!

I've included an image of something Gameknight and I built using the amplified terrain setting: a creeper prison. You can see some of them escaped and are now swimming with their guards.

The creative opportunity this program offers users is incredible, with people building entire cities, cliff hanging civilizations, and even cities in the clouds; the real game, however, is played in Survival mode. In this setting, users are dropped into a blocky world with nothing but the clothes on their backs. Knowing that night is fast approaching, users must gather resources: wood, stone, iron, etc., to craft tools and weapons so they can protect themselves when the monsters come; nighttime is monster time.

To find resources, the player must create mines, digging deep into the flesh of Minecraft in hopes of finding coal and iron, both necessities for making the metal weapons and armor essential to survival. As they dig, the users will encounter caverns, lava-filled chambers, and possibly the rare abandoned mine or dungeon where treasures wait to be

discovered—but with passageways and chambers patrolled by monsters (zombies, skeletons, and spiders) waiting to snare the unwary.

Though the land is filled with monsters, the user is not alone. Vast servers exist online where hundreds or even thousands of users play the game, all sharing space and resources along with other creatures in Minecraft. These servers host many types of gameplay, from minigames, to spleefing (my favorite), to PvP (I'm terrible at Player-vs-Player battles), to fractions, to Survival, to Creative . . . It's amazing what people have created with Minecraft, and these many, many servers are evidence of the creative potential Minecraft offers those with imaginative minds.

This game is an incredible platform for creative individuals who love to build and create, but they are not just limited to constructing buildings. With a feature called redstone, users can create electrical circuits within the game, using redstone circuits to power pistons and other devices so that complex machines can be created. People in the past have created music players, fully operational 8-bit computers, and sophisticated minigames within Minecraft, all powered by redstone. With the introduction of command blocks in version 1.4.2, command scripts could be used to control game mechanics. This opened a new creative avenue to Minecraft programs all over the world, allowing them to make even more sophisticated mechanisms in the game.

The beauty and brilliance of Minecraft is that it's not just a game, but an operating system that allows users to create their own games and express themselves in ways that were not available prior to Minecraft. With the many updates constantly flowing from Mojang, the game is continuing to evolve and get better. The creative programmers at Mojang have been expanding the instructions available for command blocks, allowing games to be constructed like Missile Wars (one of my favorites) and of course the classic, Cake Defense (another of my favorites). If you haven't tried these, you should; they are a lot of fun when played with friends. The newest update, called the Bountiful Update, has added some really cool features. My favorites are the Ocean Monument, the Guardians, and of course the rabbits. (Did you notice the last line in the update description? Interesting. Maybe he was there all along. Maybe he's still there.)

Minecraft isn't just a game, an operating system, or a computer programming environment . . . it is something more. It's like a blank canvas that extends in all directions, forever, and is filled with unlimited possibilities.

What can you create?

"We have not passed that subtle line between childhood and adulthood until we move from the passive voice to the active voice—that is, until we have stopped saying 'It got lost,' and say, 'I lost it.'"

—Sydney J. Harris

CHAPTER 1

HISSING VILLAIN

The silvery mist swirled around Gameknight999 as he walked across the featureless terrain. Faint outlines of blocky trees stood out through the shining haze, their stiff upright forms barely visible through the fog. As Gameknight approached, they seemed to evaporate, turning to smoke.

Pivoting in a tight circle, he scanned the area around him. Everywhere he saw the same thing; a silvery mist masking the features of the landscape. Gameknight999 could start to make out more shapes through the fog: another tree here . . . a grassy hill there . . . but in every case, when he closed the distance, they just disappeared.

It was strange, but also oddly familiar. He'd been here before . . . not in this land with the disappearing trees and nonexistent hills, but in this silvery mist. The memory struggled to come forth from the back of his mind, but there was also something else lurking in that memory . . . and it scared him.

"What is this place?" he said aloud to no one. "It's almost like I remember it from a . . ."

And then it came to him; this was the Land of Dreams. The first time he'd been pulled into Mine-craft—when he'd first met his friends Crafter, Hunter, and Stitcher—he had come to this place of silvery mist. Crafter had called it the Land of Dreams and had referred to Gameknight999 as a dream-walker; a person that could intentionally move through the Land of Dreams. This was the place between being awake and fully asleep, where nightmares could come to life . . .

Peering into the silvery mist, he looked for the glowing red eyes of his old enemies, Erebus and Mal-acoda. They had led the assault on Minecraft and had tried to destroy the Source, the place from which all Minecraft code originated. Gameknight and the NPCs of the Overworld had turned back the crashing tide of monsters and protected the Source, saving Minecraft and all the digital lives within. But now he was back in Minecraft again . . . this time with his sister, as well.

Suddenly, a hissing sound pierced through the fog. Turning around, he looked at the ground, expecting to find some kind of snake. But that was silly . . . there were no snakes in Minecraft . . .

The last time he'd been in the Land of Dreams, he'd been fighting for his life, locked in battle with Erebus, the King of the Endermen. That battle had nearly cost him his life, but he had triumphed with the help of his friends and countless users at his side. Now, in the silvery mist of the Land of Dreams, he was alone, completely alone, and he could tell that there was something in here with him.

Hisssssss.

There it was again!

He reached into his inventory and tried to draw his sword . . . but he had nothing with him. Then Gameknight remembered two things about the Land of Dreams: first, it was a dream world and whatever you could imagine would become real in the misty realm. Closing his eyes, he imagined he had his favorite bow, with Punch II, Power IV, *and* Infinity enchantments on it. *Suddenly, the bow appeared in his hand, waves of iridescent light shimmering along its enchanted length. The magical weapon cast a blue illumination into the mist, allowing him to see a little further ahead . . . good. And the second thing he remembered: even though things looked dreamlike in the Land of Dreams, they were real and they could hurt you. In fact, in his last battle with Erebus, the evil enderman learned that if you die in the Land of Dreams, you die for real. And that made the Land of Dreams an incredibly dangerous place.*

Hisssssssss.

As he peered into the silvery mist, some-thing materialized. It wasn't really a shape, but a color . . . purple. A single point of purple light started to form . . . then another and another until there were many spots of light floating in the mist.

What are those? *Gameknight thought.*

Taking a step closer, Gameknight readied him-self for an attack. With a thought, diamond armor suddenly materialized on his body, its crystalline surface also shimmering with enchantments. As he moved forward, the hissing returned . . . it was com-ing from those purple lights.

They grew brighter.

Could it be my old enemies, Malacoda or Ere-bus, came back to life? *Gameknight thought.* No, it couldn't be that.

And then one of the purple spots blinked. They were eyes . . . spider eyes!

The eyes grew brighter as the monster took a step closer to Gameknight, but they were not just giving off more light. No, they were giving off something else . . . hatred. These eyes hated Gameknight999 with every fiber of their being, and he could tell that if they had the chance, they would destroy him right then.

"So, I meet that User-that-is-not-a-user at last," said a voice from the mist.

"Show yourself, monster!" Gameknight shouted.

"When we are ready," the spider answered. "Why don't you come near and give usssss some nice hugssssss?"

The extended hissing-like sound of the monster's voice made Gameknight's skin crawl.

A clicking sound then came from the monster as it snapped its razor sharp mandibles together.

"I have been waiting for a hundred yearssss to meet you, User-that-is-not-a-user," the monster said. "Come, let ussssss get acquainted."

"Stay away from me, beast!"

He fired an arrow at those purple eyes, but the projectile just passed through what he thought would be the monster's head like there was nothing there. He could hear his arrow clatter to the ground far into the mist, the spider unharmed.

"Ha ha ha, that wasssss nice," the spider mocked. "Thank you for your little gift. Now, let me introduce myself. I am Shaikulud, the queen of the spiderssss, and soon I will destroy you."

The clicking of her mandibles intensified as she moved closer. Gameknight could hear the razor sharp claws on the end of each of her eight legs clicking on the hard ground as she moved forward, but her body still remained shrouded in mist.

"I have been commanded by the Maker to destroy you and your friendsssss. Once you are gone, my children will flow across the surface of Minecraft and destroy the NPCsssss once and for all. With the help of the greenssss, we will take back the world that wassss meant for ussss."

Gameknight drew another arrow and aimed at one of the hateful eyes. Releasing the arrow, he saw it fly straight for the purple-glowing spot then pass through as if it were made of smoke.

"Ha ha ha . . . that tickled," Shaikulud mocked. "You must stop your pathetic resistance and come to me so that I can destroy you."

Suddenly, clicking sounds came from all around him. Looking into the mist, Gameknight999 could see red spider eyes materialize, every one of them burning with unquenchable hatred. Drawing arrow after arrow, he fired at the red eyes. But the same thing happened: his arrows flew through them as if they were made of nothing but shadows . . . and rage. Turning back to Shaikulud, Gameknight dropped his bow then held out his hand. A shimmering diamond sword materialized in his right hand.

"If you want me, spider, then you'll have to come here and get me."

"In time, User-that-is-not-a-user, in time. But for now, I will let my daughterssss have a little fun with you." Shaikulud then raised her voice so that it resonated throughout the Land of Dreams. "Children . . . attack!"

Gameknight could hear the spiders charging at him from all sides. If he stayed here, he would be destroyed. Instead of fighting, he dropped his sword and closed his eyes. And then, with every bit of mental strength he had, he shouted as loud as he could.

"WAKE UP . . . WAKE UP . . . WAKE UP!"

CHAPTER 2

CRAFTER'S PLAN

Gameknight woke with a start. Reaching into his inventory, he drew his sword as he stood, ready for the spider attack that was not coming.

"You have a funny way of waking up," said a voice behind him.

Turning, he found his friend, Hunter, standing behind him.

She stepped toward him and carefully put a reassuring hand on his shoulder. It was dawn and the morning rays from the sun were piercing through the overhead leafy canopy, the golden shafts of light shining down on the two of them. The light made Hunter's curly red hair almost seem to glow, momentarily giving the appearance that she was surrounded by some kind of magical crimson aura. But then the sun rose a bit higher, the lighting changed, and the moment was gone.

"Are you OK?" she asked.

Gameknight looked down at his shimmering diamond sword, then up into Hunter's warm brown eyes. He could see the look of concern on her face and knew that his face must be betraying the sense of terror he felt. Carefully, he put away his sword and looked around. They were in their makeshift camp in the middle of the woods, hiding from Herobrine and his zombie horde. Looking to the perimeter of their camp, Gameknight could see the wooden barricades that had been constructed at nightfall; a temporary barrier to keep the monsters out. Glancing up to the treetops, he could see archers perched amidst the branches, their keen eyes looking for movement in the forest below.

There were no spiders attacking. It had just been a dream. And yet, maybe it had been more . . .

"Gameknight . . . what's wrong?" Hunter asked, pulling at his sleeve to get his attention. "Would you tell me what's going on? Is there . . ."

"The Land of Dreams," he said in a shaky voice.

Instantly, Hunter grew silent. She too could travel through the Land of Dreams, as could her younger sister, Stitcher. All three of them were dream-walkers, which incredibly rare in the world of Minecraft.

"What was it?" she asked in a low voice as she moved closer. "Not Erebus or Malacoda?" A look of fear crossed her face as she spoke the name of their old enemies.

"No," Gameknight answered. "Something else. A spider named Shaikulud."

"Did you say Shaikulud?" a young voice said from behind.

Turning, Gameknight found a young boy with shoulder-length blond hair approaching. He had bright blue eyes that seemed to peer straight into Gameknight's soul. But the eyes also held a look of ageless wisdom, as though they'd been in Minecraft for decades longer than possible. He wore a smock that covered him from neck to ankles, as all the villagers did, but his was colored black with a gray stripe down the center. The color of his clothing marked his position in this community: village crafter.

He was Gameknight's best friend in Minecraft, Crafter. He was the village's leader before Gameknight came into the game through the use of his father's invention, the digitizer. This device had transferred every aspect of his being from his physical body and completely transported into Minecraft. Here, within the game that was so much more than a game, he was now the User-that-is-not-a-user. His user name floated above his head, like all users, but he lacked the shining server thread that extended from the player's head and stretched up into the sky, connecting them to the servers. Gameknight999 had no server thread and was not connected to the servers because he was *inside* the server. He looked like a user, but without the server thread, he was not a user; he was something else . . .

"What was that name, User-that-is-not-a-user?" Crafter asked again.

"She called herself Shaikulud," Gameknight answered.

Crafter's face turned pale.

"You want to tell us what it means?" Hunter asked.

Even though Crafter looked like a child, he was actually one of the oldest NPCs (non-playable characters) in Minecraft. In Gameknight's first adventure as the User-that-is-not-a-user, he and Crafter had faced off against a massive army of monsters, their own army of users at their backs. During that battle, Crafter, in his old gray-haired form, had been killed in defense of Minecraft. But because he'd accumulated enough XP (experience points), he had been able to respawn into the next higher server plane, materializing in the child's body that they saw before them. Being the oldest NPC in Minecraft meant that he knew the most about its history and lore.

"The name Shaikulud comes to us from very far back in Minecraft's history," Crafter explained.

"What?" another voice asked. It was Game-knight's sister, Monet113.

She was climbing down a ladder that led up to the treetops, a bow in her hand. In the orange glow of sunrise, her midnight blue made her look like a shadow as she moved down from the leafy canopy. The bands of pale blue across her front mixed with speckles of white splattered across her chest and back were the only clue that she was not some kind of dark apparition from a dream. Her bright green eyes looked as though they were glowing in the pale morning light. She looked down on her brother with affection. But the most striking thing about her appearance was her hair; fluorescent blue locks spilled down her shoulder and back, standing out in stark contrast against her dark skin. Monet's love of color was evident in every aspect of her appearance, though the colors did little to hide her from prying eyes.

"Shhh," Gameknight said as he turned to his sister then turned back to Crafter. "Please continue."

"I was saying, the name Shaikulud comes to us from far back in Minecraft's history. My Great-Great-Aunt Brewer told us of an ancient creature that prowled the jungles of Minecraft, guarding some ancient secret."

"What kind of secret was she guarding?" Monet asked as she rubbed the sleep from her eyes.

"No one knows," Crafter replied. "The only things I remember Brewer telling me were that Shaikulud was crafted by some kind of evil being and that she was guarding the most ancient secret in Minecraft."

"Sounds exciting," Monet said, drawing an angry glare from Hunter. "What?"

"We need to stay focused and not go off on any unnecessary adventures," Hunter said, knowing just how impulsive Monet could be.

Just then, the sound of howling wolves filled the air. They had noticed an unusual number of wolves about, but they had not been attacking, just staying out of sight in the forest. One of the NPCs with them, Herder, tried to go out and bring the wolves back. As the keeper of the animals, Herder was anxious to find any stray animal and bring them under his protection, but wolves hardly needed any protection. In fact, after Herder befriended them, the wolves acted as sentries for the NPCs, guarding their perimeter and watching for monsters.

Now, Herder streaked by, running toward the howling sounds. Leaping up onto the wooden barricade the villagers had built around their camp before going to sleep, Herder shot out into the forest, hoping to find the illusive animals.

Someone laughed.

"There goes the Wolfman again," one of the NPCs said.

"I hope he can bring some back this time," another added.

Wolfman was the new name many of the NPCs had taken to calling him. They used to pick on the boy, calling him names like pig-boy, his differences drawing abuse from the bullies. But after he saved the day on the steps of the Source by arriving to the battle with a massive pack of wolves, the villagers had recognized that his differences from the other NPCs should not be mocked, but embraced. Now he was a favorite of the village, his wolves prized by all.

"Crafter, get back to your story," Hunter snapped.

"Oh yeah," the NPC continued, "anyway, this Shaikulud was an extremely dangerous creature. Great-Great-Aunt Brewer said that this Shaikulud, whatever kind of monster she was, was incredibly strong and vicious. It would be best if we could avoid tangling with her."

"We don't want to tangle with any monsters, if we can avoid it," Stitcher, Hunter's younger sister, added as she walked up to the group.

Gameknight turned and saw her approaching. She was much shorter than Hunter, but had the same curly red hair, the coiled ruby springs bouncing as she walked. But she had a look in her eyes that was very different from her sister's. Monsters had destroyed their village and killed their parents during the war to destroy Minecraft. Stitcher had been captured and taken to work as a slave in the Nether. Gameknight had been able to save the younger sister, but an angry rage still simmered within the older. Hunter had a burning desire for revenge against the monsters of Minecraft, wanting to pay them back for the suffering they'd caused to her sister and village. It was something that threatened to consume her, and it worried both Gameknight and Stitcher.

"She's a spider," Gameknight said, his voice shaking ever so slightly with fear. "The queen of the spiders, and I think she knows we're here."

"Why is it that all the monster royalty are after you?" Hunter asked playfully. "First it was the King of the Endermen, then the King of the Nether, then the Zombie King . . . now it's the Spider Queen. What is it with you that attracts all these creatures?"

"Must be my sparkling personality," he answered, then laughed an uneasy, nervous laugh.

"Anyway," Crafter continued, "we will try to avoid this Shaikulud whenever possible. Now are we ready to break camp?"

"Yes," boomed Digger's deep voice from behind.

Turning, Gameknight saw the hulking form of Digger approaching. His broad shoulders and thick arms were the results of his many hours digging in the mines for the village, and that strength had served them through the many battles they'd had over the past few days.

"Then let's get moving," Hunter added.

"But where are we going?" Gameknight asked. "Crafter, you told us about the Oracle in the jungle temple somewhere on this server, but where is she? How do we find her?"

"I've been giving that some thought, and I've come to the conclusion that we need more information in order to find the Oracle's temple."

"Where are we going to get more information . . . Google?" Monet asked.

"What's a Google?" Stitcher replied.

Gameknight and Monet laughed.

"What?" the young NPC asked.

"Nothing," Gameknight explained. "It's just something that we use in the physical world to get information. It's like all the books in the world stored online."

"That's what we need," Stitcher replied.

"We have something like that here in Minecraft," Crafter said, drawing all eyes to him. "It's the library."

"You have a library in Minecraft?" Gameknight asked.

"Yes, in fact, you've been in it before . . . remember?"

"Of course, the stronghold," Gameknight said.

"Exactly."

"A stronghold . . . what's a stronghold?" Monet asked.

"There are three strongholds on every server," Crafter explained. "They are well hidden so that only those with the correct items and knowledge can enter. Last time, we had the Iron Rose to point us to the stronghold's location, but we do not have that with us now. We must find the stronghold, somehow, on our own."

"Eyes of Ender," Gameknight said.

"What are you talking about?" Hunter asked.

"We need the Eyes of Ender; they will lead us to the stronghold."

Crafter looked at his friend, a look of curiosity and confusion on his face.

"Crafter, you don't know what the Eyes of Ender are?" Gameknight asked.

The young NPC with the old blue eyes just shook his head.

Smiling, the User-that-is-not-a-user stood a little taller as he realized that he knew something about Minecraft that Crafter did not.

"Well," Hunter asked as she punched Gameknight playfully in the arm, "are you going to tell us, or just stand there smiling like an idiot?"

"If you throw an Eye of Ender, it will fly toward the stronghold. And when you get over the stronghold, the Eye will fly straight down toward the ground. All we need is a bunch of Eyes of Ender and we can easily find the stronghold."

"Do you happen to have some Eyes of Ender with you?" Hunter asked.

"Well . . . no."

She sighed, then rolled her eyes.

"But you have some here," Monet113 added. All eyes turned to her in surprise. "What? I've been studying Minecraft and learning what I could about the game before I started to play. I know a thing or two. You have a villager here that I bet has some. Is there a priest villager here?"

"Of course," Crafter answered. "Every village has a priest NPC."

"You can trade emeralds for Eyes of Ender . . . he has them," Monet explained. "We can also craft some of them as well. Just combine some blaze powder with an ender pearl. I bet after the Last Battle on the stairs leading to the Source, you have a bunch of both?"

Crafter reached into his inventory and withdrew two ender pearls. The pale blue orbs had a dark center that looked like the pupil at the center of a cerulean eye. They looked spooky, and Gameknight shivered ever so slightly when he remembered how they'd been obtained—battling an enderman. Putting it back into his inventory, Crafter glanced at the other NPCs. They all looked at Monet, then to Gameknight, curious as to how she could know so much.

"I wrote down some notes about our last adventures and she found them . . . OK?" Gameknight said, trying to defend himself.

The NPCs glared at him, then all laughed as the guilty look on Gameknight's face grew.

"Well, you heard Monet113, the Sister-to-the-User-that-is-not-a-user . . . let's get to work," Crafter ordered.

And at once, everyone started to move, looking for the priest and gathering the necessary crafting items.

Gameknight moved next to his sister and beamed with pride; her knowledge was exactly the right thing they needed. Putting an arm around her, he looked down at her.

"I'm still mad that you for using Dad's digitizer and coming into Minecraft," he said to her.

Monet's self-satisfied smile faded a bit.

"I'm glad you're here now," he added, and her smile returned. "But you have to remember this isn't a game. The monsters here all want to destroy you, and I don't know what will happen to us if they are successful."

"You really know how to calm people's fears, brother," she said.

"Be serious," he snapped. "I'm responsible for you until we get out of Minecraft, so that means that you listen to me and do what I tell you . . . understand?"

Monet rolled her eyes . . . kind of like how Gameknight would to his parents.

"Understand?!"

"Yeah . . . yeah."

Gameknight tried to give her a cheerful smile, but the faint sound of a zombie moan from far away

tore his eyes from her. Scanning the forest suspiciously, he could imagine all the monsters waiting
for them out in the wilderness of Minecraft. The
image of those terrible, hateful, purple eyes filled
his mind, and a shiver of dread ran down his spine.

CHAPTER 3
HEROBRINE'S TRANSFORMATION

Herobrine materialized on a grassy knoll that overlooked a village, a dense forest behind him. It was quite a picturesque view; the village was nestled between two grass-covered hills, flowers dotting the terrain like little candies on two huge scoops of green ice cream. At the center of the village stood a tall, rocky structure that loomed high above the rest of the buildings. It was the watchtower and could be found in all villages. Atop the tall tower would be an NPC with the best eyesight. They would be the lookout who would watch for attacking monsters. Around the village was a cobblestone wall, a fortification left over from the Last Battle for Minecraft. It hugged the community close, with archer towers at the corners and battlements all along its perimeter. The barrier would keep out regular monsters, but had no chance of keeping out Herobrine.

Through the center of the village ran a slow moving river. The cool waterway cut through the fortified walls, but iron gratings had been installed to allow the water to flow through the village and exit through the opposite side. Its winding path continued on past the village and extended across the landscape until it disappeared in the distance. Anyone else would have found the scene quite beautiful, but to Herobrine, it was terrible.

"Why can't these NPCs live underground in the dark caves and shadowy passages?" he said aloud to no one. "That's where they should be . . . hidden away so that nobody could ever find them. Well, I'll make sure nobody finds this village ever again."

He smiled an evil toothy smile, then laughed a sadistic laugh that made the grass near his feet cringe with fear. Closing his eyes, he listened to the music of Minecraft and could feel the inner workings of the software that controlled everything on this server. In an instant he could feel his enemy, Gameknight999. Through his shadow-crafter powers, Herobrine could feel his prey as if he were a thorn on the stem of a flower. The User-that-is-not-a-user's presence echoed through the music of Minecraft like the remnants of a distant storm. Though Herobrine couldn't pinpoint his exact location, he could still feel him, and Gameknight999's very presence filled the evil shadow-crafter with a nearly uncontrollable rage.

I see that you are still here on this server, my friend, he thought to himself. *Excellent. When I feel you trying to use the Gateway of Light, I will be there and will flow into the physical world with you. Then I will take my revenge on those that imprisoned me in this game. The destruction of the Minecraft servers will come first, then the destruction of the physical world. I will turn your weapons of destruction upon you, then laugh when the users in the physical world beg for mercy and forgiveness . . . for you will get neither.*

He laughed to himself and he imagined the fear that would spread, then glared down at the village.

"But first, I must find where you are hiding, Gameknight999," he said. "Let's see how much information I can wring from the NPCs in this pathetic village."

Closing his eyes, he gathered his powers and reached out with his senses.

"Come, my children, I have need of your services!" he shouted.

Instantly, the clicking of spiders sounded in the dense forest, the scuttling of creeper feet adding to the cacophony. An army of giant black spiders slowly crawled down from the overhead canopy, scaling the vertical sides of the tree trunks as if they were impervious to gravity's gentle touch.

"Go forth, my friends, and destroy the village below!" he shouted. "Let none survive!"

As the monsters flowed down the grassy knoll, he could hear an alarm sound; someone was banging on an armored chest plate with the flat of a sword. It was likely the Watcher in the tall cobblestone tower.

The dark shadow-crafter could hear screams from the villagers below as they gathered weapons and armor to prepare for the inescapable battle that was about to descend upon their community. Closing his eyes, Herobrine teleported down into the village, materializing near the well that sat unused next to the babbling river. It was chaos in the village as NPCs ran to their defensive stations. He could see archers climbing to the top of their fortified walls, with more archers in the tall towers on the corners.

Moving to the nearest villager, he grasped him by the collar and pulled him behind one of the buildings.

"What are you doing?" the villager asked "Who are you?"

"I want to know where the User-that-is-not-a-user went, and you are going to tell me."

"What are you talking about?" the villager answered.

In the blink of an eye, Herobrine drew his diamond sword and hit the villager with it. In an instant, the NPC lost half its health. Grabbing him by the shirt again, he drew the now terrified villager up close, his eyes glowing bright with rage.

"I will ask you one more time," Herobrine said in a soft, yet dangerous voice. "Where is the User-that-is-not-a-user hiding?"

"I don't know what you are talking about," stammered the NPC.

By the look of his clothing, Herobrine guessed that this was the blacksmith and probably spent most of his time near the furnaces and forges. He likely knew nothing. Swinging his blade with all his might, he hit the NPC again, rending the rest of his HP from his body. With a *pop*, the blacksmith disappeared, leaving behind a collection of items and three balls of XP.

"I will know what is inside your head, blacksmith, one way or another."

Smiling, Herobrine stepped forward and allowed the XP to flow into him for the first time in a long time. Slowly, a pale white glow enveloped his body as the XP was integrated into his own computer code. This triggered his body to transform, slowly morphing from his previous appearance to that of his newest victim. He changed from the dark shadow-crafter wearing a midnight black smock, to a shorter, stockier NPC wearing a dark brown smock, a dusty black apron hanging from his neck. It all happened just as Herobrine expected.

He could feel the mind of the blacksmith struggle within his own brain, the captured computer code in a state of panic. They always fought back at first, but surrendered to Herobrine once they realized their fate was sealed, giving up all of their thoughts and memories.

Herobrine scanned the mind of the newly acquired blacksmith. It turned out he knew nothing about the whereabouts of the User-that-is-not-a-user.

An explosion rocked the ground; one of the creepers had detonated somewhere outside the village. Moving to the edge of the building, he glanced at the battlements. He could see all of the villagers clustered on one side. Apparently those idiotic spiders had focused their attacks on only one side . . . the fools.

They'll have to just fend for themselves for a little bit, he thought. *I need to find out where my enemy is hiding . . . that's more important than destroying this village.*

And then a thought came to his mind . . . not one of Herobrine's thoughts, but one of the newly consumed blacksmith's. The thought consisted of a single word, but it rang with desperate truth.

Crafter.

Of course, I'll question their crafter.

Looking across the village square, he could see the crafter on the fortified wall. He was directing the archers to concentrate their shots on strategic targets, making their defense a coordinated effort. Teleporting to him, Herobrine materialized at his side. Surprised, the crafter turned toward him.

"Blacky, what are you doing here?" the crafter said. "You are supposed to be watching the south wall."

Grabbing him by the shirt, Herobrine brought out his sword and attacked the crafter with all his might. Before any of the other NPCs could react, he consumed the crafter's HP. Disappearing with the faintest of sounds, the crafter left behind all of his crafting tools and three balls of XP. Stepping forward, Herobrine could feel the XP flow into him, filling him with knowledge and power. His body then began to glow with an eerie, menacing radiance as his body flowed into something else, his form momentarily indistinct. Some of the other villagers saw the attack and yelled out, but none were brave enough to approach.

As the transforming glow faded, the villagers saw their crafter standing there, looking unharmed, and they were confused. Herobrine's eyes glowed with excitement as the crafter's thoughts flowed into his mind. But with startling certainty, Herobrine realized that this crafter knew nothing. In fact, this whole village knew nothing about the whereabouts of the User-that-is-not-a-user . . . and this made him angry, terribly angry.

As his eyes glowed with hatred, he disappeared from the fortified wall and appeared next to a creeper. Laying his hand on the creeper's shoulder, he disappeared again and reappeared within the village, the creeper teleporting with him. Moving the green-spotted monster next to the fortified wall, he gave the creature a command . . . the only command these dumb creatures really understood.

"Detonate," he ordered.

Instantly, the creeper glowed bright, slowly expanding as the ignition sequence began. Stepping back, Herobrine watched with glee as the creeper exploded, tearing a massive hole in the fortified wall.

"Come forward, my children, and obey the Maker!" Herobrine yelled to the spiders and creepers.

At the sound of his voice, thirty spiders flowed through the break in the wall like a shadowy flood. Then the creepers scuttled into the village, their little pig-like feet moving in a blur, looking for targets to destroy.

Smiling a satisfied smile, Herobrine teleported out of the village and back to the grassy knoll. Looking down on the scene with glee, Herobrine's eyes glowed bright with evil joy as the sounds of shouts and screams reached his ears. This village would be erased from the surface of Minecraft and the inhabitants forgotten.

Glancing down at his new clothing, he could see that he was still garbed in the traditional clothing of a village crafter; he wore a black smock with a gray stripe running down the center. *An expected side effect I could use to my advantage*, he thought.

"I'm coming for you, Gameknight999," he said aloud to no one . . . to everyone. "Let's see if you recognize me now."

With an evil laugh, Herobrine disappeared.

CHAPTER 4
SURPRISE ATTACK

Gameknight walked through the forest with his sister at his side, his shimmering diamond sword in his hand. Turning his head from side to side, he looked for monsters that could be prowling about. The other NPCs seemed at ease, for the sun was up. But in this roofed forest biome, the interlocked branches high overhead cast an almost continuous covering of shade throughout the forest . . . and that meant the zombies could attack at any time.

Looking to Monet, he could see that she had her bow out and was practicing shooting arrows at trees, Stitcher at her side. The young NPC had taken it upon herself to teach Monet113 how to shoot, and Gameknight's sister had picked it up quickly, showing that she was actually a pretty good archer. Behind his sister walked Tiller, the NPC who had adopted Monet as her own daughter. During the first battle for Minecraft, when Erebus and the monsters of the Overworld had fallen upon their village, Tiller's daughter had perished during the fighting. The old woman had never fully recovered from the loss until Monet's arrival. Now she doted on her at every opportunity, making sure she was fed and warm, and focused all of her attention on Monet like a tireless, dedicated parent.

"Nice shot, dear," Tiller said.

Monet turned and looked at the old woman, then smiled as she drew another arrow from her inventory.

Tiller was a field worker; her job was to prepare the fields for planting. She wore a dark brown smock with a light brown stripe down the center, like all did in her trade. As she walked behind Monet, her shoulder-length salt-and-pepper gray hair, now mostly salt, bobbed up and down, framing her smiling face and warm hazel eyes.

All of the villagers had taken to Monet instantly, partially because she was the sister of the User-that-is-not-a-user, but also because she was a free spirit who saw beauty in everything she encountered . . . the color of the sky at sunset, the texture of zombie skin when bathed in moonlight, the sparkling of the morning dew on spiderwebs . . . Anything and everything was beautiful to her eye, and her appreciation for their surroundings was contagious even though they were in constant peril.

Monet had entered the game just a few days ago, and she basically had no items in her inventory other than the clothes on her back. Many of the villagers gave her things that she needed: a crafting bench, a pickaxe, a shovel, an ax, a sword . . . Everyone was quick to give her something. But the thing she loved the most was the gift from the blacksmith. Smithy had been able to scrounge up enough iron to make her a full suit of armor. She had been so excited to have her own armor that she tried it on right away. Of course, the first thing she did was paint it, wiping splashes of bright yellow across the front, then adding streaks of green and red, a blushing of pink down the arms and legs, blue across the waist. She was a walking rainbow who brought a smile from every NPC who looked upon her. It was as if she'd made this work of art for them, to bring a little bit of beauty into this perilous adventure, and they all appreciated it.

Looking down at her now, Gameknight was confused. His sister did not seem the least bit afraid of their current situation. They were being chased by the most terrible and evil monster in Minecraft . . . Herobrine. In fact, she seemed completely unaware of the danger. Maybe Monet was incredibly brave, or maybe she was just a kid and didn't understand what was at stake. Gameknight wasn't sure.

Ahead of them, Gameknight could see that the roofed forest was ending and they were moving out into the open plains.

"The trees have provided good cover," Gameknight said, "but I will like getting out of all this shade."

"Do we have to go this way?" Monet asked.

"We have to go the way the Eyes of Ender tell us," Gameknight explained. "That's the way to the hidden stronghold."

At the head of the column, Gameknight could see Crafter and Digger. They were throwing Eyes of Ender into the air and following the direction they flew, Digger doing the throwing with his massive arms, and Crafter doing the spotting. They threw one every hundred blocks or so, trying to conserve their supply so they wouldn't run out. The glowing orbs continued to point the party toward the rising sun, always to the east.

As they moved out of the forest and onto the rolling plains, Gameknight had the strange feeling that they were being watched. He kept glancing to the rear of the column.

"What's wrong?" Monet asked.

"I don't know . . . this just feels funny," Gameknight replied. "I want you to stay close to Stitcher; I'm going to the back of the army."

"I want to go with you," she complained.

"No . . . just do what I say," Gameknight snapped. "This isn't a game, and I have to make sure that everyone here is safe. They're all here because of me, so I have to be certain there's no danger."

"Come on dear," Tiller said, a cautious tone to her voice. "Let's get up to the front where it will be safer."

Monet113 looked at Tiller and smiled, then turned and gave Gameknight a pouty, disappointed look.

Ignoring her attempts at getting him to reconsider, the User-that-is-not-a-user turned and ran to the back of their formation. He could hear Stitcher giving commands to some of the other warriors, instructing them to follow. They all did as Stitcher commanded partially because of the respect the soldiers had for her prowess with her bow, but also because they all feared Hunter, her older sister. In a few seconds, one of the soldiers rode up to Gameknight with a horse for him. Without asking, the User-that-is-not-a-user leapt up into the saddle and pointed the horse to the rear. As he rode, he noticed that more and more of the cavalry were following him. He stopped his mount at the edge of the forest and waited until all the villagers were out of the forest, then slowly he followed the slowest of the villagers, making sure they were well protected.

As they moved away from the tree line, he heard a sound and spun his horse around. On the treetops, he could see dark figures sunken down amidst the leaves, the leafy foliage hiding their bodies but their multiple red eyes gave away their presence . . . Spiders, and lots of them.

"We're under attack, everyone run!" Gameknight shouted.

The villagers, battle hardened from the constant attacks on their village and the attacks in the forest, did not yell or scream; they just drew their weapons and waited for commands.

"Keep moving away from the trees!" he yelled. "They aren't attacking yet, but they will soon."

Crafter and Digger came running up, with Hunter close behind.

"What's happening?" Crafter asked.

Gameknight pointed at the treetops.

"They're probably waiting for more spiders, or instructions from their leader," Crafter explained. "Spiders are solitary animals and do not like working together. They only do it when they are forced, so if the order hasn't been given yet, they won't move."

"We need to take advantage of this," Digger said in his deep voice. "Ahead is a hill, with rivers on either side. It would be a good, defensible position."

Turning, Gameknight looked at the terrain and understood what Digger meant. Ahead, the ground slowly sloped upward, forming a large mound around which two rivers flowed, then met behind the hill, forming a watery V that protected their rear. That would be a good place to set up a defense.

"Digger, I need you to get the people moving as fast as you can." He then dismounted and drew his sword. "Warriors, get off your horses and give them to the elderly and weak. We will be the rear guard while the rest of the village gets on that hill."

Without questioning the order, the soldiers jumped off their horses and found another to ride them. They then returned with weapons drawn to stand at Gameknight's side.

"Digger . . . go!"

The big NPC turned and ran off, shouting instructions to everyone else. Before Crafter could leave, Gameknight grabbed his sleeve.

"Crafter, you remember the little surprise we had for the monsters during the battle at the Bridge to Nowhere, after we had retrieved the Iron Rose?" Gameknight999 asked.

Smiling, Crafter nodded his head.

"Great-Uncle Weaver would like you," the young NPC replied, then turned and ran off, yelling commands of his own.

"What . . . what?" Monet asked, she had just gotten to Gameknight's side. "Who's Great-Uncle Weaver?"

"He was Crafter's Great-Uncle, and he said once, 'Many problems with monsters can be solved with some creativity and a little TNT,'" Gameknight said. "Crafter is going to prepare a little surprise for these spiders." And then he gave his sister an angry glare. "What are you doing here? You should be heading up the hill to safety."

Glancing back up the hill, he could see Tiller waving and running toward her.

"I'm going to help you fight," she answered. "You saw how good I'm shooting now with my bow."

"Don't be ridiculous, Monet, this is going to be dangerous. War is not for kids."

"But you're a kid."

"Not in Minecraft," Gameknight snapped. "Here, I'm the User-that-is-not-a-user, a seasoned warrior and you're still just a kid. Now get back there where it's safe."

"NO!"

Gameknight sighed, then motioned for the blacksmith to come near.

"Smithy, please escort my sister to the hill with the rest of the villagers," Gameknight instructed. "If she refuses, then pick her up and carry her. She can't stay here. I . . . ahh . . . need her to help set up the defenses . . ." He leaned forward and stared into the eyes of the big blacksmith. "Do you understand? I can't focus on protecting my kid sister while an army of spiders is about to attack."

Smithy nodded, then grabbed Monet's hand and started walking quickly toward the hill. Monet sighed, then turned and followed the big NPC, a look of disappointment on her face.

Grinning a satisfied smile, Gameknight could hear Tiller lecture his sister on the dangers of monsters, while Monet objected to her mistreatment. He was glad that Tiller was there; it made it a little easier to focus on keeping everyone safe from the monsters of Minecraft. Turning, he faced the forest and peered into its shadowy depths. As he drew his sword from his inventory, a voice spoke to him.

"You could have been a little nicer about that."

Turning, he found Stitcher next to him, scowling up at him, her unibrow furled with anger.

"What do you mean," Gameknight replied. "She can't be down here, she's just a kid."

"I'm just a kid," she replied. "Should I go back with the old women and hide?"

"Of course not, Stitcher, I need you here. Besides, that's different. You're not a kid . . . you're Stitcher. We've fought side-by-side through a hundred battles, and I know you can take care of yourself. But Monet is too young and not experienced enough yet. I can't trust her to be smart out here on the battlefield."

"Something's happening!" one of the warriors yelled.

Turning back to the tree line, Gameknight could see more spiders on the treetops. As their numbers swelled, their agitated clicking grew in volume, the sound resembling a swarm of a million angry crickets. Through the leaves, the growing number of bright red eyes glared at them with a burning hatred that seemed so intense that Gameknight could almost feel the heat from their stares. This shocked him. These spiders hated the NPCs with such a passion that it was almost consuming their ability to think.

What would cause these monsters to hate NPCs so much? he thought.

"Everyone start backing up," Gameknight commanded. "Draw your bows and get ready. Form two ranks and spread out. We can't let the spiders get past us, no matter what. The warriors behind us need more time."

The warriors cheered, then put away their blades and pulled out their bows. Fitting arrows to bowstrings, the warriors continued to move backward, arrows pointed at the monsters in the distance. Through the trees, Gameknight could see movement. Something green and spotted was moving between the tall oaks, creatures scurrying along on tiny little feet. As they moved to the edge of the trees, Gameknight could see what they were . . . creepers.

Great, more monsters.

Stepping forward, Gameknight turned and faced the warriors. Looking into their scared faces, he saw pride in their eyes, but also terror. They could see they were completely outnumbered, and fighting a horde of spiders out in the open was never a very good idea. But with all that going through their minds, they looked to Gameknight with hope and the expectation that he would save them.

Their lives are in my hands . . . They're relying on me for their survival.

Whether he wanted to or not, he was the User-that-is-not-a-user, and he needed to figure out a way for these NPCs to survive the upcoming battle. And as he glanced at the spiders that were gathering on the treetops, Gameknight could feel there was a solution there that would save his friends' lives. And then he had an idea . . . *the creepers, of course.* In his mind, he moved the green spotted monsters out onto the battlefield like they were pieces on a chess board. He imagined the other pieces: the spiders, the villagers standing at his side, the villagers on the hill behind him . . . they slowly came together into a strategy that just might save their lives.

"OK, here's what we're going to do," Gameknight yelled. "When the monsters charge, front rank will . . ." and he explained his plan to nodding heads.

When he completed his orders, Gameknight could see hope shining bright in their boxy faces— they all now had a chance to survive the impending battle.

"Here they come!" one of the soldiers yelled.

And as Gameknight turned to face the impending mob, that old familiar feeling spread through his body. It was a sensation that made his feet feel as if they had been planted in concrete and his arms feel weak. It made him uncertain if he was doing the right thing, or if his decisions would get everyone killed. It was a feeling that he'd felt so many times in Minecraft that it had become an old friend . . . or maybe a nemesis.

It was fear.

Pushing the fear aside, he focused on *the now* and gripped his sword firmly, then turned and faced the storm of monsters rushing toward them. With every bit of strength he had, he yelled out his battle cry and it echoed across the battlefield.

"FOR MINECRAFT!"

CHAPTER 5

BROTHERSSSS AND SISTERSSSS

Turning, Gameknight999 saw a large group of creepers stream out of the forest, their tiny feet a blur as they moved. Adding to their numbers, a dark wave of spiders slowly climbed down from the leafy canopy. Their black bodies hugged the tall tree trunks as they moved down the vertical blocks like huge shadowy drops of lethal rain.

"Everyone back up and wait until they get in range!" Gameknight yelled as he continued to walk backward. "Show no fear, for you have friends and neighbors at your side. Your village is a family, and family always looks out for each other." He took a few more steps backward as the spiders and creepers drew closer. "This battlefield is ours and we aren't going to let a bunch of monsters take it from us."

"Yeah!" shouted Stitcher, her high-pitched child-like voice piercing through the clicking of the spiders and making the other warriors smile.

"Ready," Gameknight yelled. "NOW!"

The front rank of warriors dropped to one knee, and then as one, all the warriors drew back their arrows and fired. They aimed for the creepers that were at the front of the charge. They only needed to ignite one. The arrows streaked through the air, their pointed tips finding both creepers and spiders, but none of them caused the creepers to explode. Apparently these creepers were better disciplined than those in the past.

Fitting arrows to bowstrings, the small collection of warriors fired as fast as they could. Another wave of arrows flew through the air and landed amidst the green spotted creatures . . . nothing. Gameknight growled in frustration. The spiders were getting close, dangerously close.

But then one lone flaming arrow streaked across the sky. It sailed high overhead, having been fired from far behind their formation. As it flew, Gameknight could see the waves of iridescent blue magic sparkling along the shaft, the tip burning red with enchanted flame. Looking back, he could see Hunter running to his position.

Pausing, she fired another one, then continued to sprint. The first arrow hit a creeper directly in the chest. The magical flame made the green monster glow white as a hissing sound filled the air. Then the second arrow landed in its shoulder, making it glow even brighter. In an instant, the monster exploded, tearing a great hole into the landscape and throwing many of the other monsters into the air. Gameknight could see the creepers nearby were now glowing white as they fell to the ground, then exploded in a punctuated chain reaction that carved a deep gouge into the grassy plain. Explosions echoed across the landscape as the remaining creepers finished the last instances of their fiery lives.

At least we stopped the creepers, Gameknight thought.

And then the spiders charged forward.

"Keep moving back!" Gameknight yelled. "Front rank, draw swords. Archers aim for the cave spiders."

Stepping forward, Gameknight put himself in front of Stitcher and glared at the oncoming wave of monsters, daring any of them to try to get by and hurt his friend.

That's not gonna happen! he thought.

He could feel the weight of responsibility for all these lives standing at his side, but wasn't sure how he would deal with it if any of them were hurt. He was sure that some of them would get injured or killed . . . it was battle. Right now, however, he knew that he couldn't give that any thought. Right now, it was time to fight, and that was something that Gameknight definitely knew how to do.

The front wave of spiders crashed down upon the NPC warriors. Swordsmen slashed at the fuzzy black monsters as their shining curved claws reached out to touch flesh. In front of Gameknight was the hate-filled face of a giant spider. It slashed out, but Gameknight was able to easily block the attacks. Countering, he swung at the monster, faking to the left, then attacking to the right. He tore into the monster's HP, his sword cutting with ferocity that filled the monster's eyes with fear. Not letting it escape, Gameknight pressed his advance as Stitcher's arrows flew over his shoulder and sank into the monster's side. In seconds it disappeared with a *pop!*

Screams of pain on both sides filled the air as NPCs squared off against spiders. The archers behind the rank of swordsmen kept firing their deadly missiles from between NPCs, focusing their shots on the blue cave spiders amongst the attackers; the spiders' deadly poison something to be feared. Gameknight was glad there weren't more of them. The archers focused on trying to hold back the flood of violence, but there were just too many monsters.

Warriors dropped as their HP was consumed, their inventory falling to the ground alongside balls of silk as spiders also met their fates.

We can't continue to lose one NPC for each spiders . . . we'll end up defeated.

"Pull back . . . pull back!" Gameknight yelled.

The warriors, understanding Gameknight's plan, moved backward, yielding ground to the monsters. This made the clicking from the spiders even louder as their excitement grew.

Backing up even faster, the NPCs continued to fight, but now they were backing up the hill, slowly getting closer to the rest of the villagers.

"Keep fighting, but pull back," Gameknight yelled. "We can't hold our ground against these spiders . . . pull back!"

The massive wave of spiders approaching them was like an unstoppable flood. Gameknight could hear the villagers behind him now, Digger and Crafter yelling out orders and organizing their defense.

"Ready!" Gameknight shouted.

The warriors fought harder, trying to slow the advance of the monsters.

"READY!" he shouted even louder.

The swordsmen suddenly surged forward and hacked violently at the closest spiders.

"NOW!"

The ranks of warriors suddenly split in the middle and ran to the sides, exposing the center of the battlefield and giving the spiders a clear view of the villagers on the hilltop. The spiders clicked with glee, thinking the NPCs were retreating, but then the clicking suddenly stopped when they realized they were staring straight into a line of TNT cannons.

"FIRE!" yelled Crafter.

The clear blue sky was suddenly filled with thunder.

BOOM! The cannons' blocks exploded, launching flashing cubes of TNT into the air. They fell amidst the spiders and detonated, tearing up landscape and spider bodies. Before the spiders could figure out what to do . . .

BOOM!

Another volley of TNT blocks were launched into the air and exploded within the spider horde. As the monsters scrambled about, the warriors on the sides of the battlefield quickly slipped behind them and then closed in, sealing off any avenue of retreat.

BOOM!

Indecision ruled the spiders' minds. They all turned and started to retreat, but found two ranks of swordsman at their rear. As they stood there trying to figure out what to do, the warriors from the hilltop charged forward. In an instant, the battle changed: the spiders, once the hunters, were now the hunted. NPCs from the hilltop surged forward as the swordsmen at the rear attacked.

Gameknight, at the head of the charge, swung his diamond blade as if it weighed nothing. He hit spider after spider, his sword just an iridescent blur as he dove into the battle. Watching those on his side, he frequently aided his neighbors as they did the same for him, their swords sometimes slashing at the same spider. As he fought, he could see his sister on the hilltop, her bow in her hand. She fired arrow after arrow into the center of the spider cluster. Her missiles sank into spider bodies as if guided there by a computer. Her aim was nearly flawless.

Next to him, he saw a young NPC fall to one knee as spider claws tore into this leg. Gameknight started to move to his side, but Tiller was already there, her wrinkled arms wielding her sword with lethal efficiency. She swung it, not as fast as most, but she was painfully accurate. The spider stepped back from the young NPC as her iron blade bit into the monster's side.

"You leave our children alone!" she screamed at the beast.

As the youth recovered from the blow, he stood and fought at Tiller's side, each guarding the other's back.

"It's not nice to slash at villagers with claws!" Tiller shouted at the spiders.

That made Gameknight briefly smile.

Moving from the pair, the User-that-is-not-a-user found more targets. Slashing at spider after spider, he was lost in the haze of battle, his body moving on pure instinct. The only thought that flashed though his mind was *Please don't let any of them die.* And so he moved like a razor sharp whirlwind, spinning from one monster to the next without pause, protecting his friends—and him-self—from the butcher's bill.

In minutes, the monster horde had been reduced to only a handful of creatures, then only two, and then only one lone spider. With its HP nearly depleted, the monster fell to the ground, its eight long legs sticking straight out to the side. Moving quickly, the warriors grabbed some rope and tied up the monster so that it could not escape. Game-knight's last instruction had been to save one for questioning.

He was about to approach the monster when he heard a moaning wail come from one of the NPCs. Turning his head, he saw Tiller on her knees before a pile of items that had once been in someone's inventory. Moving to her side, Gameknight put a reassuring hand on her shoulder.

Turning, Tiller looked up at him, tiny boxy tears flowing down her cheeks.

"Who was it?" Gameknight asked.

"Young Cobbler," she replied. She put her face in her hand and wept for a moment, then looked back up at Gameknight999, her hazel eyes now streaked with red. "She was a good girl, almost the same age as my beautiful daughter, Rider, when she was killed." She stopped speaking as uncon-trollable sobs of grief raked over her.

Suddenly, Monet113 was at her side, putting her arm around the woman and hugging her tightly.

"Why do they . . . hate us so . . . much?" Tiller said between sobs, speaking to Gameknight999, to everyone.

Slowly she picked up all the items and stuffed them in her inventory, then stood and raised her hand high over her head, fingers spread wide. Instantly, all the other NPCs did the same, the battlefield now sprouting boxy hands that slowly clinched into fists.

I let one of them die, Gameknight thought to himself as he did the salute for the dead. He squeezed his hand so tightly that his knuckles started to pop and crack. *I should have been there next to Cobbler. I should have protected her, but instead . . . I failed.*

Grief crashed down on him like a tidal wave. It was his responsibility . . . and he failed.

How do I handle this? I never asked to be a hero, I only wanted to be a kid. I'm not . . .

Suddenly, Tiller was standing before him, handing him a loaf of bread.

"Cobbler would have wanted you to have her bread," she said, tears still streaming down her cheeks. "She would have wanted you to stay strong so that you can defend Minecraft and all of us."

The woman carefully distributed the rest of the young girl's belongings amongst the villagers. With the acceptance of each gift, the villagers became angrier and angrier.

Click . . . click . . . click . . .

The captive spider clicked its mandibles together. It sounded like the equivalent of laughter. Drawing his sword, Gameknight stepped closer to the monster. They needed information, for on the battlefield, knowledge was power. Monet113 stepped to his side.

The spider looked up at the two of them, then swiveled one eye to look up over their heads.

"There are two User-that-is-not-a-userssss," the spider said in a screechy hissing voice. "The queen will know of thissss soon."

"Why are you attacking us?" Gameknight asked. "Answer me truthfully and I will let you live. What is your name?"

"I am called Shakal," the spider answered, then glared up at Gameknight999. "The Sisterssss and Brotherssss are commanded by the Maker to hunt down the User-that-is-not-a-user, but we were not told that there were two."

Gameknight turned and looked at his sister, then glanced at Crafter, who was now approaching the monster.

"He doesn't know that your sister is here," Crafter said. "Apparently Herobrine doesn't know everything."

"The Maker commandssss the queen, and the queen commandssss the Sisterssss. We have been instructed to hunt down the Maker'ssss enemy." The spider then swiveled her eyes to glance about at the gathering crowd of NPCs. She strained to take another breath, the continued. "You will all be destroyed soon, and then the Maker will destroy the User-that-is-not-a-user. Your destruction issss inevitable."

"It doesn't have to be that way," Monet113 said. "We don't have to fight. It's possible to live together even though we are different. There are always things in common that we could explore together."

"NPCssss and spiderssss can never live together. We know of the terrible thingssss NPCssss do, we know of your hatred toward ussss. There are too many differencessss . . . there can never be peace. Now kill me and be done with it."

One of the warriors lifted his sword, but Gameknight stopped him with a raised hand.

"No, we won't kill her," Gameknight said as he turned to look at the crowd that now encircled the monster. "I said she could live if she talked with us, and I have to keep my word." Kneeling, he brought his face up close and looked into her multiple burning red eyes. "You must tell your queen that there is another way, other than violence . . . that there can be peace. Our mercy toward you and letting you live is evidence of our intent for peace. Do you understand?"

She clicked her razor sharp mandibles together. Their sudden, lightning fast motion startled him and made him move back.

"Release her," Gameknight ordered.

"I'm not so sure that's a good idea," Hunter said from behind him.

Turning, he found her standing on a block of dirt near the back of the crowd.

"We have to show them that we mean what we say . . . that peace is better than war."

She sighed.

"There can never be peace with monsters," she said in a low, cautious voice, hoping the spider could not hear. "There are too many differences, too many things we do not understand. Peace requires a common ground for us to understand them. Look at that monster . . . there is nothing there that is like us. They are hideous and dangerous. They have nothing in common with us, and they never will. Peace with the monsters of Minecraft is a dream that will never come true."

"But we must try," Gameknight said, then turned back to the crowd. "Release her."

Digger stepped forward and sliced through the ropes with his pickaxe.

The spider gathered her legs under her and looked furtively at the crowd that surrounded her.

"Make way so she can leave," Gameknight instructed.

The crowd parted so the spider could make her way back to the forest.

Her burning red eyes glanced at the forest, then swiveled back to Gameknight999. Each eye went in a different direction, surveying the crowd around her. Turning, she faced the opening and took a step toward the forest, then spun and sprang into the air. She headed straight toward Monet. The dark claws at the end of each leg were pointed straight toward her head. Gameknight was too far away to do anything, and all the other NPCs had sheathed their swords. There was nothing he could do but watch.

And then a flaming arrow streaked through the air and hit the spider in mid strike, followed by another. With a *pop*, the spider disappeared, a handful of silk thread landing on her intended target, Monet113.

Gameknight turned and found Hunter aiming her bow at the place where the spider had disappeared, another arrow drawn back, ready to fire.

"You see," Hunter said, almost shouted. "They cannot be trusted!"

Gameknight ignored her comment and rushed to his sister's side. Pulling the strands of spider silk from his sister's shoulders, he could see that she was shocked, a look of confused terror on her square face.

"That monster wanted to kill me," Monet said, her voice cracking with emotion.

"Welcome to Minecraft," Hunter said softly, but not soft enough.

Gameknight glared at Hunter as she stepped off the block of dirt and put away her bow, then turned back to his sister.

"How are we going to ever get out of here?" Monet113 asked, her voice now, finally, filled with fear.

"I don't know, Monet, I don't know."

CHAPTER 6
LOOKING FOR
HIS NEMESIS

Herobrine approached the village from a distance. He didn't want to startle them or tip them off to his real identity. Concentrating for a moment, he tried to push all of his violent, evil thoughts deep down into his subconscious, doing his best to fill his mind with peaceful images. As he did this, the glow around his eyes slowly faded, giving him a normal, NPC look.

He still held the appearance of the last villager he'd destroyed and absorbed their XP. He'd changed into the shape from which the XP came, not just in appearance but in every aspect. Herobrine actually *became* that person. He could choose not to transform, but only by avoiding the XP. It was some kind of cruel joke that the Minecraft server software played on him; he didn't really understand it, but he'd found long ago that it had its benefits. Herobrine had used this to his advantage many times in the past, avoiding detection by that old hag in the jungle more than once. Today, he would use his changed appearance to draw information from the idiotic NPCs in the village.

I'll find you yet, Gameknight999!

Walking down the sandy hill that led toward the desert village, he swerved around the tall green cacti that dotted this desert biome. Far out in the distance, he could see where a savannah biome met the desert. The strange, jagged acacia trees leaned this way and that above the pale green grass that stretched into the distance. In the other direction, the sandy desert stretched until it met the horizon, green cacti decorating the landscape. He preferred the desert biomes where there were fewer trees, for that meant safety for Herobrine; the old hag had a more difficult time sensing him.

Increasing his pace, Herobrine started to run toward the village. He had to show the proper amount of desperation as he approached. Sprinting forward, he could hear an alarm being sounded, the Watcher in the tall watchtower banging on a piece of armor with the flat of their sword. Armored heads instantly popped up along the fortified sandstone wall, cautious eyes surveying their surroundings.

"Open the gates!" someone shouted.

Herobrine smiled.

As the metal doors creaked open, his face showed the right amount of happiness and relief. Lone villagers like himself typically had little chance of survival out in the open, so Herobrine knew that he had to look relieved. And he was . . . not because he was finally safe, for no creature in Minecraft could truly harm him. No, he was relieved because of all the information he'd be able squeeze out of these fools.

One of the NPCs approached him; it was the village crafter. He wore the normal clothing: black smock with a gray stripe running down the center. This one was not as old as he would have expected. With a full head of dark hair and the faintest wisps of gray encroaching near the edges, this NPC seemed to be just barely out of adolescence.

"Are you Lost?" the crafter asked.

The Lost were villagers who no longer had a village crafter. When a village's crafter died or was killed unexpectedly, crafting powers were often not transferred to another NPC, and the village had trouble staying together. When this happened, the villagers usually left the village to strike out in random directions across the Overworld until they found a new home. Most did not survive this trek.

"That's right," Herobrine lied, trying to sound meek. "Our crafter was taken from us by a group of spiders. I headed out as all of the NPCs were required, looking for a new village and a new crafter."

"Well, you found a new village and are welcome with us," the crafter replied. "Come, let me bond you to me." Crafters used their powers to establish a connection between themselves and new villagers.

"Please, not out here in the open," Herobrine said. "Let us go somewhere private."

The crafter nodded and led Herobrine through the village. They walked across the open square, past the village's well and their fields of crops. Moving past the tall sandstone tower that sat at the center of the community, Herobrine looked up and thought how wonderful it would be to see that tower destroyed. As these images flitted through his mind, he could feel his eyes starting to glow, and instantly pushed the thoughts away.

I have to be careful! he reminded himself.

Looking away from the tower, he stared at the back of the crafter as they moved between the buildings, his smock brushing the sandstone walls. It looked as if they were heading for the blacksmith's shop; he could see the line of furnaces on the stone porch. Moving directly to the front door, the crafter opened the door and stepped inside. As the NPC stepped to the back of the room, Herobrine went in and closed the door behind him.

Taking a few steps forward, Herobrine positioned himself between the two windows that were set into one wall and waited. Turning, the crafter looked up at Herobrine, then stepped forward and rested his hand on the newcomer's shoulder. As the NPC gathered his crafting powers, Herobrine drew his diamond sword. His eyes wide with confusion, the crafter tried to ask a question, but the diamond blade came down on the NPC with vicious efficiency. In just a few hits, the crafter was gone, the floor littered with his possessions: multiple crafting benches, tools, an iron blade, some bread . . . and three glowing balls of XP.

Stepping forward, Herobrine let the items flow into his inventory. Looking down, he watched the spheres of XP slowly seep into his feet. In that instant, a panicked voice filled his mind, the voice of the village's crafter.

What's going on . . . what happened . . . am I . . .

You are mine, Herobrine thought, then gave a maniacal laugh. Allowing his eyes to glow for an instant, he let the newly absorbed mind see his true self.

Oh no . . . moaned the crafter from within Herobrine's mind . . . *it can't be.*

Herobrine laughed again, then started to sift through the new memories in his mind. Pushing the crafter's personality aside, he buried the fabric of the NPC's personality deep within his subconscious and allowed him to wallow in the darkness with the other beings Herobrine had absorbed over the centuries.

And then he found it!

Here was the memory that he was looking for.

"I was out hunting for food," a hunter said to the crafter, "and I saw an entire community of NPCs leaving their village. They were following what looked like a user wearing diamond armor, but the armor was cracked and damaged. It looked like he had been in some kind of terrible battle. Anyway, I noticed that the user didn't have a server thread . . . Was that the User-that-is-not-a . . ."

"Quiet!" the crafter said, then glanced around to see if anyone was listening.

Pulling the hunter by the sleeve, he moved into the nearest building; it was the baker's house. Stepping into the home, he found the baker at the back of the room, tending to the furnaces that were cooking loaves of bread for the community.

"Can you please give us some privacy, Baker?" the crafter said. "I must talk with Hunter for a moment."

The baker bowed to his crafter then moved outside. The hunter watched the baker walk across the room, his smock covered with flour, and move outside. Reaching out, he pulled the door shut, his long sandy-blond hair swished across his face as he turned to face his crafter.

"Now tell me everything," the crafter commanded, a serious look to his square face.

"Well, I saw all the people leaving their village, the User-that-is . . . ah . . . you know . . . leading them into the forest. There was a young boy next to him, but he

was dressed as you are, in the clothing of a crafter. I was confused. They couldn't have a crafter that was only a child . . . anyway, I watched them go into the forest, moving quietly as if they didn't want to be noticed. The last person I saw leave the village was another hunter like me, but this one was a woman, and she had long curly red hair. I thought this was all kinda strange and came back to tell you right away."

"You did the right thing, Hunter," the crafter said as he placed a reassuring hand on his strong shoulder. "But you must not tell this to anyone. We must take this information to our graves if necessary . . . do you understand?"

The hunter nodded, his blond hair bouncing up and down.

"Good."

"So, you found him for me," Herobrine said quietly to no one.

He could hear the screams from the crafter deep within his mind, but ignored the voice. The crafter would give up soon enough. They always did.

Stepping out of the blacksmith's house, Herobrine moved back to the open square at the center of the village and scanned the faces of those milling about. He saw builders, weavers, milkers, diggers . . . and then he saw him. The hunter was standing on top of the fortified wall that surrounded the village, his bow in his hand, arrow notched.

Closing his eyes, he teleported to the NPC and appeared right behind him. As he turned, Herobrine reached out and tore the bow from his hand. Throwing the weapon aside, he could hear the screams of shock from the other NPCs, but Herobrine was not concerned; the time for stealth was over.

Drawing his sword, he brought it down on the defenseless NPC, tearing into his HP until it was extinguished. The hunter disappeared with a *pop!,* leaving behind a scattering of items and three glowing balls of XP. As he stepped forward to retrieve the XP, Herobrine could hear the alarm sounding from atop the watchtower, but again he didn't care. These pitiful beings could not hurt him.

Turning to glare down at the villagers, Herobrine let his eyes glow bright, then he disappeared, teleporting to the nearest nest of spiders. As he reappeared, his eyes were still glowing bright, giving notice to any spiders nearby. One of the large, black monsters failed to notice the eyes and reached out to attack what looked like a defenseless villager. Herobrine disappeared just as the wicked black claws reached out for his flesh. He materialized right behind the monster, his sword already moving. The diamond blade crashed down on the creature before it knew what was happening. Swinging it with all his might, he slashed at the spider over and over, carving away at the creature's HP. After three well-timed hits, the spider vanished, leaving behind a ball of silk and three small shimmering spheres.

Quickly, he moved away from the glowing balls of XP; he didn't want to turn into a spider . . . ever. Teleporting again, he reappeared at the center of the large cave that held this nest of spiders. Their clicking filled the space with a thousand castanets, but as soon as they saw his eyes, the mandibles stilled, bringing an eerie calm to the chamber. Moving to a nearby spider, he placed his hand on her fuzzy back and disappeared, taking the eight-legged monster with him.

He materialized on the sandy hill that overlooked the village, the spider right next to him. The villagers below instantly saw him and his companion. The alarm sounded again, even though Herobrine could tell the village was still in a state of confusion.

"You and your sisters are to destroy that village below," Herobrine said to the monsters. "Do you understand?"

"But the defensessss . . . the wall . . . we cannot get over that wall."

Herobrine looked down at the fortified wall and could see that the villagers had placed upside-down steps around the edge of the wall so that they jutted out around the perimeter, creating an overhang that was not scalable by the spiders. These villagers were smart . . . all the more reason to destroy them.

"Do not concern yourself about the wall, it is insignificant."

Reaching out, he placed his hand on her back again, then closed his eyes. They disappeared from the hilltop and materialized between the buildings and shops in the village. Most of the NPCs were on the walls, readying their defenses . . . fools.

As his eyes glowed brighter, Herobrine left the spider and teleported away, then reappeared with another spider. He then disappeared again and reappeared with another . . . and another . . . and another. Using his teleportation powers, Herobrine brought fifty of the sisters into the village. Their bodies pressed together in the narrow alleyway between the buildings, their mandibles kept still, avoiding detection.

"These NPCs are planning on attacking your queen for no reason other than they hate all spiders," Herobrine said in a low voice, his eyes glowing bright, lighting up the hunter's face and sandy-blond hair. "Now go forth and destroy them before they kill your queen."

The spiders charged forward, spreading out through the village. They fell on the unsuspecting NPCs quickly, taking advantage of their element of surprise.

The village didn't stand a chance.

Herobrine appeared on the sandy hilltop again and looked down on the doomed community. He could hear screams of panic and terror come from behind the fortified walls, and smiled even more, his eyes glowing like two tiny evil suns. Closing his eyes, Herobrine sorted through the memories of the hunter until he found those he needed.

"I have found your trail, User-that-is-not-a-user," he said in a loud, booming voice. "Soon, you will be on your knees before me, begging for mercy . . . something that you will never receive."

Herobrine then laughed an evil, maniacal laugh that made the nearby cacti seem to cringe. With his eyes burning bright, he disappeared from the sandy hilltop, pursuing his nemesis, his eyes the last thing to fade from view.

CHAPTER 7

GREAT NEPHEW BUILDER

The village woke from another restless sleep. They had moved through the rolling hills of the grassland and entered this birch forest just before sundown. Working as quickly as they could, the NPCs had built their fortifications just before the first attack had come. It had been a small collection of zombies, about eight of the decaying monsters charging their position. The archers in the trees had easily put down the attack; none had escaped. But that was just the beginning. Monsters had harried them all night, zombies and spiders and creepers trying to sneak up on them through the darkness. The archers that Hunter had placed in the trees managed to hold the monsters at bay while the cavalry rode out to meet the threats, but it had been a constant state of alarm that kept everyone on edge. Hardly anyone managed to get any sleep.

Gameknight was worried.

The number of monsters attacking had not been very great, only handfuls of creatures at any one time. What worried Gameknight was that these creatures were willing to attack when outnumbered ten-to-one. They seemed to be overwhelmed with hatred for the NPCs, as if driven by some kind of external force. He could imagine Herobrine's hand in this somehow, and as the image of those glowing eyes surfaced in the back of his mind, Gameknight shuttered.

Suddenly, a ray of sunlight pierced through the leafy veil overhead and brought him back to the present.

It was sunrise!

Turning to look at the NPCs around him, he could see them all breathe a sigh of relief as the sun's square face peeked over the horizon. Its warm presence drove away the inborn fear they all had of the night and filled them with hope. Smiles now spread across square faces as the brightening sky drove away the scowls of fear.

"Break camp . . . let's get moving!" Digger yelled.

The big NPC had taken command of the villagers, keeping them moving and focusing on the daily chores of finding food and water and a place to camp each night. He was a natural leader, his booming voice able to get people moving at a moment's notice. Gameknight watched Digger and was envious. He seemed comfortable with the responsibility of making sure everyone was taken care of and safe. The responsibility fit him like a glove.

He hated being the User-that-is-not-a-user, being responsible for saving all of their lives and coming up with plans to keep them safe, while at the same time figuring out how to defeat Herobrine. The responsibility was too much.

He laughed to himself.

He was always telling his parents that he wanted to be treated like a big kid, that he wanted to take on more responsibility and show them that he was mature and reliable. So his dad had given him some more responsibility: "Take care of your sister while I'm on my business trips," he'd said to Tommy. "Make sure that she's OK and safe."

It turned out to be too much responsibility.

His father didn't understand how hard it was: problems at school, problems with the neighborhood kids, and now with problems in Minecraft. It was just too much for him to do. He hated it when they treated him like a little kid, but now he realized he didn't really like having all that responsibility either. Really, he wanted to be in-between—a kid when it was the right time . . . and responsible when it was needed. Being all grown up was too much right now.

A flash of curly red hair flickered out of the corner of his eye. Turning, he saw Stitcher heading out into the forest, an arrow fitted to her bowstring. Trailing about ten steps behind, he saw Monet113 following.

"Monet, where are you going?" Gameknight shouted.

"I'm going to help Stitcher check the surroundings for any stray monsters," she replied as she turned and faced him.

"No, you need to stay here, where it's safe," he replied, an angry scowl on his face. "Stay in the camp and don't go out into the forest . . . it's dangerous."

"But Stitcher is . . ."

"I don't care, you need to stay here where it's safe."

"But I can take care of . . ."

"NO!" Gameknight snapped. He then turned to find the blacksmith amidst the sea of square faces.

"Smithy, Monet will help you pack up all the tools and furnaces. Please make sure she helps you and stays in the camp. Feel free to throw her over your shoulder if needed."

The squat NPC that always seemed covered with ash brought his fist firmly to his chest. A cloud of dust billowed from his apron with the salute and settled to the ground, coloring the grass at his feet with a subtle gray hue.

"Grrr," Monet growled, her frustration showing plainly on her boxy face. "Sometimes you're just like Mom and Dad!"

The comment stung, but he knew he had to keep her safe, and he couldn't do that with her running around out in the forest; she was just a kid. As everyone gathered their belongings, he considered that comment. *Was* he like Mom and Dad? No, he wasn't like his dad, because his dad was never around. His dad always left Tommy with all of his responsibilities.

The community of NPCs had become very efficient at their new nomadic life. In minutes, they had all their belongings packed and defenses dismantled and were ready to move.

"All is set," Digger yelled out. "Everyone move out!"

Moving to the front of the column, Digger threw an Eye of Ender into the air as far as he could. Archers on the treetops watched it move, the glowing orb streaking off toward the rising sun.

"Still to the east," one of the archers shouted.

Digger nodded, then struck out in that direction, the entire village of NPCs following close behind.

Suddenly, Gameknight found his friend Crafter at his side. Trailing behind him were many of the villagers. They felt comfortable and safe near their crafter. Soon, Monet was at Crafter's side. She leaned forward so she could see her brother and give him an angry scowl.

"I'm not a kid!" she growled.

Gameknight ignored the comment and turned to face Crafter.

"You said you had a distant relative who'd traveled to this stronghold?"

"His name was Builder and he was my Great-Nephew. For some reason, he was always getting into trouble when he was younger . . . going on dangerous adventures with the other village kids."

"Sounds familiar," Gameknight said, glancing at his sister.

She ignored him and kept her gaze straight ahead.

"Builder decided that he wanted to find the stronghold that was supposed to be somewhere near their village. He must have had a supply of Eyes of Ender, for he somehow knew where to look. All the other kids in the village heard what he was doing and wanted to go with him, but when the parents found out, they went straight to Builder's parents. He was in big trouble and was forbidden to go."

"Did he?" Monet asked.

"Of course he did," Crafter answered. "Builder had a stubborn streak in him that he learned from his mother, Milky."

Gameknight recognized the name and remembered the story Crafter had told him long ago.

"The next night, he snuck out of the village. Twenty other kids went with him and . . ." Crafter looked like he was about to cry, his voice cracked with emotion.

Monet reached out and placed a reassuring hand on his small shoulder. Crafter patted her hand with his and continued.

"We aren't really sure what happened next," Crafter said after clearing his throat.

Gameknight took a moment to check his surroundings, looking for any danger. They were still moving through the birch woods, but he could see the forest thinning out in the distance, snow starting to cover the ground. There were no monsters nearby . . . for now. But he knew this could change at any second.

"Why?" Gameknight asked.

Crafter cleared his throat again, emotion showing clearly on his square face.

"Because Builder was the only NPC child to survive the trip," Crafter said loud enough for everyone to hear. "And when he returned, he was so terrified and guilt ridden that he eventually lost his mind."

"Oh no, that's terrible," Monet said.

"All the other kids were . . ." Tiller started to say with a sob.

Crafter nodded.

"None were heard from again," the young NPC said in a solemn voice. He held his hand up high, fingers spread wide. Many of the other villagers did the same, all of them giving the salute to the dead. "After years of questioning, the villagers were able to piece together a story, though much of it still makes no sense."

"What happened?" Gameknight asked as his eyes scanned the trees again.

"The villagers determined that Builder must have been going through an ice spikes biome when he found the stronghold," Crafter explained.

"Why do you think it was an ice spikes biome?" Gameknight asked. "Those are very rare."

"He said something about the twin pillars of ice pointing the way. It seemed likely that he was in an ice spikes biome, and there must have been two towers of ice near the stronghold."

As he spoke, the villagers moved out of the forest and started to cross snowy rolling hills. Instantly, Digger sent out riders in all directions to check for monsters. None of the NPCs liked being out in the open like this; they preferred places that were defendable, and the open plains were anything but that.

Everyone in the village was completely silent as they moved across the snow, their square feet making the snow crunch underfoot. He could see many drawing their weapons, expecting monsters to come charging over the tall hill in front of them, but as the riders returned with smiles on their faces, the NPCs relaxed a bit.

"Crafter, please continue," Gameknight said as he put away his own sword.

"OK . . . well, Builder apparently found something near the ice twins. He also said something about the twins pointing to the father, but nobody ever figured out what that meant. Anyway, somehow he found the entrance to the stronghold and went in.

"As we all know, strongholds can be dangerous places. There are always lots of monsters about and it's easy to get lost in the maze of passages. And for some reason, they are always near lava ravines or deep crevasses. We don't know what he found at this stronghold, but he kept saying something about jumping a lot. My Great-Uncle Carver thought that he meant some kind of extreme parkour, but nobody was sure. What they *were* certain of was that Builder was scared out of his mind, literally, and never came to his senses until the day he died."

"Did he say anything else about the stronghold?" Gameknight asked.

"He did say one thing over and over," Crafter said, "and everybody figured that this was what scared him into insanity."

He paused for moment as the company came to the foot of the large hill. The Eyes of Ender were saying that they had to climb the hill. Digger sent a group of soldiers up to the top of the hill to make sure zombies weren't waiting for them on the other side. As the warriors jumped up the blocks and climbed the hill, the rest of the NPCs waited at the bottom, catching their breaths.

"Well," Hunter shouted, her voice piercing the silence and shocking everyone a little. "What did Builder say?"

"Oh yeah," Crafter mumbled. "What was I saying . . . OK, I remember . . . he used to mumble something about . . . the swarm."

"The swarm?" Monet asked, her colorful armor standing out against the white snow that frosted the ground, her fluorescent blue hair spilling out from under her helmet. "What was that supposed to mean?"

"Nobody could ever figure that out," Crafter answered. "My grandfather, Grampa Carver, who was just a boy at the time, told me once that he thought it was some kind of mob that attacked him and destroyed all those other kids, but nobody really knew for sure. In the end, they knew only two things for sure."

"Everyone, come up here!" yelled one of the warriors who had climbed the hill ahead of them. "You all have to see this!"

Moving as one, the NPCs started to climb the hill.

"Well?" Hunter asked.

"What?" Crafter responded.

She let out an exasperated groan. "What two things did they learn?"

"Oh yeah . . ." Crafter continued, "the first thing was a sad thing; those other kids were never heard from again. And the second thing was that Builder hadn't been afraid of anything before that trip to the stronghold, so whatever it was that scared him that much . . . it must have been horrific."

They all considered Crafter's words as they climbed the hill, Gameknight mulling over what he had learned. When he reached the top, he was still looking down at his feet, trying to puzzle out the meaning of Crafter's story. But the sound of gasps from everyone brought him back to *the now*. Drawing his sword in a fluid movement, he readied himself for battle. When he looked up, he didn't see spiders . . . or zombies . . . or creepers. Instead, he saw gigantic crystalline towers of ice reaching up toward the sky, the glacial blue standing out against the soft white snow. They were ice spikes, thousands of them.

Looking around, Gameknight realized that they had just entered the ice spikes biome, and in the distance he could see two gigantic spikes that must have stretched up at least forty blocks if not more, their features looking identical.

"The Twins," someone said next to him. Turning, he found Herder standing at his side, three wolves trailing behind him, the rest of the pack guarding the perimeter. White boxy clouds of steam billowed from his mouth when he breathed, the arctic air making its presence known. Gameknight could feel a chill settle over his body, the brisk cold nibbling on his ears and cheeks.

"Must be," Monet replied from his other shoulder.

Gameknight looked at the mighty ice spikes with awe. As if they were two gigantic frozen daggers trying to stab at the sun, they stretched straight upward, each no more than ten blocks from its brother.

"Look there," Crafter said, pointing past the twins.

In the distance, they could just barely make out the presence of an even larger ice tower that dwarfed the twins with its height and breadth.

"That must be the Father that Builder referred to," Hunter said, her breath creating square clouds of mist as she spoke.

Digger moved near the cluster of villagers and threw an Eye of Ender into the sky. It streaked straight toward the Twins and the Father in the distance.

"At least we know we are heading in the right direction," Digger said and he put away the rest of the Eyes.

"But not what we face when we get there," Gameknight added as he shivered, not with cold, but with fear.

CHAPTER 8

SHAIKULUD

Herobrine materialized in front of Crafter's village, the iron doors that led past the fortified wall standing wide open, the walls and watchtowers abandoned. Turning, he surveyed the surroundings, looking for any sign of life—there was none. Moving through the door, he stepped into the village and gazed about at the empty buildings. In front of him was a large open area with tall towers placed here and there . . . archer towers; they had been used in the defense of this village against the King of the Endermen, Erebus. At his feet, he could feel the rough gravel blocks that covered the area. Beneath this layer of gravel lay a deep pit filled with water. By activating the right redstone circuits, Herobrine knew that these gravel blocks would fall away and trap any invaders in the pit below. That annoying User-that-is-not-a-user had used this quite effectively during that first historic battle for Minecraft.

The glow from his eyes grew bright as he thought about his nemesis, Gameknight999. He had to find him and force him to use the Gateway of Light.

"I will not be trapped in this ridiculous game for one instant longer than necessary," he said to no one.

Scowling, he moved quickly through the village, confirming that no one was there. The hunter had been correct; they were all gone.

Closing his eyes, Herobrine teleported out onto the plane that stood before the village's walls, reappearing right where he'd fought Gameknight999. Smiling, he thought about the look of terror and defeat that had covered the User-that-is-not-a-user's face when his enemy realized that Herobrine could not be defeated. It had been delicious.

But then his smile turned to a frown when he looked out at the forest and saw nothing, no villagers . . . no Gameknight999. Staring down at the ground, he could see where the villagers had struck out for the forest, the matted grass still bent over from the trampling of all those feet.

"At least I know what direction you are heading . . . northeast," Herobrine said.

But he knew that the trail would quickly disappear within the forest.

What are you up to, Gameknight999? he thought.

Closing his eyes, Herobrine silently disappeared and materialized in a dense jungle that butted up against an extreme hills biome. Looking out across the landscape, he could see steep hills stretching high up into the sky as if they'd somehow been pinched and molded by gigantic fingers. The sheer faces of these hills were unscalable, their sides just too steep, forcing those that moved through this area to travel along the narrow ravines that snaked their way between the tall mountains.

Turning around, he glanced at the jungle that sat nestled against this sharp, hilly terrain. It was the densest jungle he'd ever seen, with jungle-wood trees scant three or four blocks apart. Vines hung down from the overhead canopy, draping over everything and giving the jungle the appearance that it was actually just a single gigantic leafy plant. Glowing behind the vines, he could see the bright brownish-orange cocoa pods. They stood out like little orange lanterns against all the green that filled the jungle.

"Trees . . . so many trees," Herobrine growled.

Too many for me to destroy, he thought to himself.

He could feel the sneaking eyes of the old hag within those leaves and knew he was being watched.

Fine, let her watch!

"That's right, go ahead and watch, old woman!" he shouted to the trees. "Your end draws near."

He then turned away from the jungle and walked toward the nearest mountain. It stood not more than ten paces from the edge of the jungle, its steep face made of rock and dirt with a sprinkling of coal ore here and there. At the base of the hill stood a huge opening to a dark tunnel that plunged downward into the bowels of the mountain. Standing before the entranceway, Herobrine thought it looked something like the yawning maw of some kind of subterranean beast. Pulling out a stack of blocks, he reached up and placed a few cubes of stone here and there, adding boxy teeth to the mouth and making the entrance look a little scarier.

Stepping back, he admired his work. The tunnel now looked more vicious . . . more terrifying.

Herobrine smiled.

Putting the blocks of stone back in his inventory, he moved into the tunnel. The sounds of innumerable spiders filled the stony passage, their clicking echoing off the shadowy walls. This was Shaikulud's nest.

Moving quickly through the rocky passages, he followed the tunnel's winding path as it descended deeper and deeper into the depths of Minecraft. The tunnel branched, separating into two tunnels. Moving to the intersection, Herobrine could clearly hear the clicking spiders in one of the tunnels and instantly could tell which way to go. Continuing his journey, he moved through intersection after intersection. He knew that these extreme hills biomes always had huge cave systems. That was something that he liked about these types of terrains.

The sounds of spiders grew louder and louder and he went deeper underground. They liked it where it was cold and damp; far from the level of lava, but also far from the surface. That middle zone was the spider zone, and that was his destination. Moving faster, Herobrine started to use his teleportation powers to traverse long straight tunnels where he could see his destination. He hadn't been in Shaikulud's nest for a long, long time and was uncertain if he could teleport to her cavern. If he missed and teleported into solid rock, then . . . he wasn't sure what would happen and didn't want to find out. Moving faster and faster, Herobrine started to sprint as the clicking sounds grew to the volume of a thousand castanets. Turning one last corner, he was there.

The tunnel had led him to a massive chamber, probably as large as any zombie-town, with a ceiling that stretched up at least fifty blocks high. Everywhere he saw spiderwebs, the white fluffy structures standing out against the dark stone walls.

Each web seemed to hold an egg shaded black with red dots adorning the surface. Herobrine knew that these were the next crop of spiders to be produced in this nest. Throughout the chamber, he could see with his glowing eyes the smaller cave spiders tending to the eggs. They were the males in the nest, the Brothers. The larger black spiders were Sisters.

Some of the spiders charged at him, thinking he was some kind of foolish, suicidal NPC, but as they approached with their sharp curved claws extended, Herobrine let his eyes flare bright, filling the massive chamber with light. Instantly, the spiders stopped their attack and lowered their heads, bowing to their master.

Suddenly, the clicking of the spiders stopped. At the center of the cavern, Herobrine could see a black spider larger than all the rest slowly lower herself to the ground on a long thread of silk. This spider had the look of age about her, with patches of gray hair spotting her fuzzy skin, a look of ancient fatigue on her face. She had the same bodily form as the other spiders, however, her eyes glowed an evil purple instead of the normal menacing red of the Sisters and Brothers. But the eyes weren't just bright and purple. As with all Herobrine's creations, the eyes glowed with a frightening radiance that spread out across her face. It gave this spider queen the appearance of something sinister and evil, as if her creation was for only one purpose . . . to make others suffer.

Herobrine smiled.

"Come here, Shaikulud," Herobrine said as he stood in his position, waiting for her to come to him. "We have much to discuss."

The spider moved carefully around the multitude of eggs that were scattered across the cavern floor. As she moved, the smaller cave spiders, the Brothers, scurried out of the way, making room for their queen. When she reached Herobrine, she lowered her head and bowed.

"What issss it that the Maker commandssss?" Shaikulud said.

"You will send out your spiders to search for the User-that-is-not-a-user," Herobrine commanded. "I want to know where he and his village are hiding. When you find them, you are to report to me."

"The Maker'ssss commandssss will be obeyed."

"Events are rapidly converging," he continued. "I can feel all the pieces in this game coming together just as I have foreseen. When the new hatchlings arrive, there will be enough spiders to destroy all the NPCs and claim the Overworld for spiders everywhere."

"What of the greenssss?" Shaikulud asked.

Herobrine knew that she was referring to the zombies.

"They will help in this matter . . . I have commanded it. As we speak, they are using the zombie-portals to come here from the other servers. Soon we will have a massive army of zombies that will aid in the spiders' war."

"Not spiders'sss war . . . the Maker'ssss war," Shaikulud corrected.

Herobrine nodded, then turned to look up at all the eggs that were attached to the walls and ceilings.

"Send some of your best scouts out to pass to word. The search for the User-that-is-not-a-user must start NOW!"

The spider queen bowed her head, then turned and spoke to the nearest cave spider.

"Son, bring me Shalir, Shabriri, Shintalli, and Shaxal."

The small blue spider moved off, scurrying into the shadows. In a minute, he returned with four giant spiders, each looking especially vile and dangerous. This made Herobrine smile.

"My daughterssss, you are to spread the word to the other nestssss," Shaikulud commanded. "The User-that-is-not-a-user issss to be found. Hissss location issss to be reported to me. No livessss shall be spared in thissss venture. Issss thissss understood?"

All four of the spiders clicked their mandibles together as they bowed their heads to the spider queen.

"Now go!" she commanded.

The four spiders scurried to the cave opening, then shot up into the tunnels that led to the surface, some of them crawling along the ceiling while others moved on the walls and floor.

"Well done," Herobrine said as he turned back from the entrance to face the spider queen. "It is now more important than ever that you guard the old hag and make sure that none reach her. I feel that her part in this is not complete yet, and she may still be useful to us. I created you to guard her a century ago, now you must fulfill your task and guard her well. Do you understand?"

Shaikulud bowed her head in acquiescence, her purple eyes glowing bright.

"Excellent," Herobrine said. "Now go tend to your eggs and send out the sentries to guard the hag in her stone hut. Let no one reach her and punish those who try."

"The Maker'ssss commandssss will be done."

Turning, Herobrine faced the cave opening, then allowed all of his anger and hatred for his enemy to build, causing his eyes to flare bright.

"You won't hide from me much longer!" he shouted.

And then he gathered all of his powers and reached into the very fabric of Minecraft, yelling with all his might, "I'M COMING FOR YOU GAMEKNIGHT999!"

Herobrine then disappeared, pursuing his prey.

CHAPTER 9

THE SPIDER'S WEB

The NPCs moved across the ice spikes biome in complete silence, the only sound being that of their feet crunching through the thin layer of snow on the ground. Fingertips tingled as the cold air bit at exposed skin, putting everyone a little on edge, but not just because of the temperature. They were all nervous. Being out in the open and visible from so far away was dangerous, and none of the NPCs liked this. They knew that if one monster spotted them and reported their location, then they likely would have a massive horde of monsters to contend with. As a result, the party moved between the snowy hills of this biome, following a winding path toward the two identical ice spires, the Twins. When they entered this strange land, the Twins had been far off in the distance, but now, after a hard day's march, they loomed high overhead, just around the next bend.

Gameknight walked near the front of the assembly, followed close by Monet113 and Stitcher, Crafter at his side. Suddenly, he stopped as he felt something echo through his entire being. It was a sensation that stabbed at him as if it were sharp and jagged, with rusty points tearing into his mind. At first, he thought someone, or something, had shouted is name, but it wasn't a sound as much as it was a feeling . . . a very, very bad feeling. He could sense it through the fabric of Minecraft, the music of the server planes suddenly becoming dissonant and strained. Chills ran down his spine as he started to shake with fear.

And then the feeling was gone.

"What is it?" Crafter asked as he put a hand on his friend's shoulder.

"Ahh . . . nothing," Gameknight lied as he rubbed his hands together to generate a little warmth.

"It wasn't nothing and you know it," Monet said. "I can always tell when you lie, and you always do that thing."

"Do what?" he asked.

"Ahh . . ." his sister answered, imitating her brother.

Gameknight looked away, his square cheeks turning bright red.

"I though I felt something," he explained, "you know, through the music of Minecraft. It felt like something violent and hateful was reaching out toward me."

"It was Herobrine, I'm sure of it," Crafter said. "Only he would have the power to do that." Glancing around, he could see the base of the Twins just ahead, two large hills on either side of them. Some smaller spires of ice dotted the hillsides, their glacial blue structures standing out against the snowy ground. "This would be a good place to camp for the night. It would be defendable."

Gameknight looked around as well, then nodded his head. Instantly, the NPCs started to work, setting up camp as they had done every night since leaving their village. Gameknight took his sister by the hand and climbed the nearest hill, getting out of the way of the villagers and letting them do their jobs. Once they reached the top of the hill, they sat on a block of frozen dirt and faced to the east, toward the gigantic ice spike in the distance . . . the Father. It loomed high in the air, the irregular shape twisting and turning as it soared upward, the top of the spike bulging outward, becoming twice as thick before it narrowed again and came to a point.

They sat there, admiring the many ice sculptures that dotted the landscape while the sun gradually settled to the horizon, casting a warm crimson glow. A gentle breeze blew from the east, the cold wind seeming to drive the sun to its evening resting spot. It froze the siblings a bit and caused them to move closer together for warmth. Turning around, the brother and sister watched the sunset. As if on cue, the sky started to darken from its bright blue to a darker navy, a line of orange just emerging from the tree line in the distance.

"The colors are really spectacular, don't you think, sis?" Gameknight asked, his words floating out on square steamy clouds of breath.

He received no answer. Turning, he found his sister's face mesmerized as she watched the parade of colors, the frozen sculptures before them reflecting and refracting the colors in every way possible. The landscape turned from an ice blue and snowy white canvas to a painter's palette covered with subtle colors and hues, each icy block and snow-covered patch reflecting the overhead display.

The sun settled a little lower, now only half its square face visible.

The sky changed to a deeper, darker blue with a scant few stars starting to show their shining presence far to the east. At the line dividing the sky from the ground, it was a battle between oranges and blues; the horizon looked to be lit aflame with every shade of orange and yellow and red, the space above it now a dark shade of blue. The clouds that continued to drift on their never ending trek to the west looked like fluffy white rectangles as they disappeared in the distance. They stood out in bright contrast against the navy sky but slowly darkened as they moved farther away.

The sun sank even lower, now just the barest sliver of its luminous face still visible over the horizon.

Monet gasped in wonder as the sky turned darker and darker, allowing the stars overhead to pierce through the dark veil of night, adding a sparkling climax to the colorful symphony. The horizon flared with one last gasp of orange fire, then faded to black as the sun disappeared.

It was night.

Gameknight turned to look at his sister. He saw a huge smile painted across her face, reaching from ear to ear. A small blocky tear followed a curving path down her cheek, then dripped off her chin and landed on the ground, instantly freezing.

"I bet you want to paint right now?" he asked.

She turned her head and nodded.

"But I ran out of flowers to make dye," she said, her voice sounding a little sad.

Looking around, Gameknight could see that there were no flowers sprouting out of the ground in this frozen land.

"It will have to wait until we get out of this biome," Gameknight said. "But we'll find some soon. Come on, let's see if the camp is ready."

Standing, they carefully walked down the hillside. Gameknight was surprised to find the camp finished; the efficiency of these NPCs never ceased to amaze him. A wall of dirt blocks was now erected around the camp, with towers of wood and sandstone positioned here and there to give archers a clear field of fire. Atop the taller hills, he could see Watchers standing on some of the looming ice spikes, giving the guards a clear view of the area.

At the center of the camp, Gameknight saw Herder finishing work on a corral, many of his animals already inside, clustered together for warmth. He had a strange way with animals; they all seemed to do whatever he commanded. His knowledge of the animals was unsurpassed, even with Crafter . . . he was the perfect person to care for the village's herd. Standing nearby was a large pack of wolves, each with a red collar, the animals completely bonded to the lanky youth.

Near the animal pen, Gameknight could see a field of beds that had been placed close together, their inviting red blankets standing out in stark contrast against the blocks of snow and ice. This was where the villagers not on duty would sleep. Seeing the beds, Gameknight's mind seemed to stop its resistance to the overwhelming fatigue that had been nipping at him for hours.

"Come on, Monet, let's get some rest."

"But I was going to go out with Stitcher and explore the ice spikes," she complained.

"Absolutely not," Gameknight answered, his voice stern. "Stitcher is going out on guard duty, not a sightseeing trip. And you are too young and inexperienced to stand watch."

"But Stitcher is just as small as I am. Why can she go out and not me?"

"There isn't a monster in Minecraft that would accuse Stitcher of being small when she has her bow in her hand," Gameknight999 explained. "She is a better shot than just about anyone, besides her sister, and she has faced down many a monster in battle. I have faith that Stitcher knows what she is doing."

"But not me . . . right?"

"You're too young and not ready yet!"

"I never thought I'd see the day," Monet said, sounding frustrated.

"What do you mean?"

"I never thought I'd see the day when you'd sound just like our parents: 'You're too young . . . you don't know what you are doing . . . you aren't responsible enough . . .' Just like Mom and Dad."

Before Gameknight could answer, she spun and headed to one of the beds far from him. As he stood there, shocked and hurt by her comment, she took off her armor and put it on one of the armor stands near the head of the bead. Lying down, she turned and looked at her brother, then scowled and drew the red blanket over her, instantly falling asleep.

Am I really that bad? Gameknight thought. *I know that I fight with Mom and Dad about not being treated like a kid, that I want more responsibility. But with that responsibility comes a price . . . you have to follow through even when it's hard.*

He looked at his sister lying there, asleep. Could he trust her to go out on guard duty and take on the responsibilities that all the other NPCs were doing? She was so impulsive sometimes, acting without thinking . . . that's why they were stuck here inside Minecraft. She'd used the digitizer to come into the game without thinking about the consequences of her actions. And now they were both trapped . . . because of her!

Growling in frustration, he moved to the field of beds and laid down. Gameknight kept his armor on, so he could respond quickly if they were attacked and rested his head down on the white pillow. It was not comfortable, lying down in his armor. All the places where it was cracked and chipped from the last battle with Herobrine seemed to dig into his skin, the cold diamond coating reminding him of that fateful encounter.

He started to think about that last battle, when Herobrine had almost killed him, but his body's fatigue finally won over, and in seconds he was asleep.

A silvery mist swirled about him, obscuring the terrain and hiding everything from his vision. Instantly, he knew that he was in the Land of Dreams, the space between wakefulness and complete sleep. As dreamwalkers, Hunter and Stitcher seemed to embrace this responsibility, the sisters going frequently into the Land of Dreams to ensure that everyone was safe. Monsters prowled the misty lands and could attack those who accidently appeared within the silvery fog; if you died in the Land of Dreams, you died in the waking world as well. But for Gameknight, this was just another heaping of responsibility that he'd rather not have.

Moving forward, Gameknight could see something in the distance. As he neared, he found that it was a jungle biome, with tall junglewood trees spaced close together, their branches draped with vines. Nestled within the branches, he could see glowing orange cocoa pods. Their seeds could be used to make cookies and would keep you alive when food ran short.

He could use a cookie right now.

And then he felt a cold chill that bit through his armor and shook him to the bone. It wasn't just a breeze, it was something else, something sinister and evil. Turning, he walked toward the source. Suddenly he found himself facing a series of steep hills, instantly recognizing them as an extreme hills biome. Carved into the closest of the hills was a large tunnel that yawned open like the mouth of some kind of gigantic beast. He could see blocks of stone that had been clearly placed around the edge of the entrance to look like teeth.

Why would someone do that? he thought.

Moving into the tunnel, he followed the ice-cold sensation through twisting tunnels and rocky passages. He knew that huge cave systems could always be found in the extreme hills biome, but he'd never explored one . . . until now.

After a few minutes, the tunnel opened into a gigantic cavern, probably as big as that which housed zombie-town. The far side of the cave was not visible, masked by the silvery fog. This made the hollow structure seem even bigger. Stepping into the cavern, he looked at the walls. For some reason they looked like they were moving . . . writhing and squirming as if alive.

He was scared.

Reaching into his inventory, he drew his enchanted sword. The iridescent blue radiance from the blade lit the surroundings with a sapphire glow, allowing him to see the walls more clearly.

Spiders . . . the walls were covered with spiders!

They were everywhere, on the ground, on the walls and ceilings. But more disturbing were the eggs. There must have been a thousand eggs distributed throughout this chamber, black and red ones being tended by hundreds of blue cave spiders. And somehow, he could feel through the Land of Dreams that there were hundreds of spider nests like this one across the servers. If all these eggs hatched, they would overrun everything and destroy all the NPCs, and that's if they didn't lag out the servers and make them crash.

What would happen if the server crashed? *This thought made little square goose bumps form down the back of his neck.*

Just then, a huge object lowered itself from the ceiling, hanging on the thin piece of spider silk. He couldn't see the creature well, its body still obscured by the silvery mist, but he could make out some features. Eight sharp, curved claws stuck out from the bottom of the mist, somehow sparkling in the darkness. He could not make out the body, though he assumed it was another spider. But he could make out the eyes . . . and there was something terrible about them. They glowed with a purple light that looked angry and hateful. They shone in the same way that the zombie king's had . . . and the King of the Endermen . . . and the King of the Nether. All of these creatures, Xa-Tul, Erebus, and Malacoda, had all been cut from the same cloth; all crafted by Herobrine, and now it seemed that there was another. But this one felt more dangerous than the others, as if it had been created with only one purpose in mind . . . to destroy.

"I see you have met my oldest creation," said an evil voice.

Turning, he could see Herobrine on the far side of the cave, his unmistakable eyes glowing bright with hatred. He was not clothed in black as he had been that last time they met; he looked different. The green smock with a brown stripe made him look like a hunter. The long sandy-blond hair that hung around his shoulders, coupled with his tall frame, made him look totally different, but the eyes showed his true self.

"This is Shaikulud, my first creation," Herobrine said. "I'm going to make sure you become well acquainted with her. You should take a good look at her now, for when you meet, you will likely not have the opportunity to appreciate her beauty."

Gameknight turned back to look at the spider. Her body was still obscured by the mist, but as he reached out with his mind, he saw thin purple curving threads stretch out from her eyes. The lavender filaments shot out in all directions and wrapped themselves around each individual spider. It was as if she were the puppet master, controlling all of the spiders with her very will.

Gameknight looked back at the queen and noticed that some thicker strands of glowing filament shot up to the rocky ceiling and pierced the stone roof as if it were not there. He wondered where those purple fibers went . . . maybe to more spiders somewhere else, or maybe to the many nests that were hidden in the shadows throughout Minecraft. But before he could really give it any thought, Herobrine's voice filled his mind.

"You will not elude my grasp for long, User-that-is-not-a-user. My lovely pets will find you soon enough, and then we will face each other again in battle."

"I'm not afraid of you, Herobrine!" Gameknight shouted, but his voice cracked with fear.

Herobrine laughed.

"When we meet, you will do as I command and take the Gateway of Light back to the physical world. You have no choice."

"Never!"

"Ha! It is inevitable. When you feel your last heartbeat and draw your last breath, you will claw and scratch at anything that could save your miserable life, for you lack the strength to resist me. The skin that you wear is of a full-grown user, but I can see within you and I know that you are but a child. You don't have the guts to make the hard decision and stick to it."

He laughed again, somehow sounding even more evil.

"Soon you will be mine," Herobrine said. "But for now, I think we'll have a little fun."

Drawing his own diamond blade, Herobrine disappeared and materialized right next to him. Gameknight could see the shadow-crafter raise his sword and swing it at him.

Without attempting to block the attack, Gameknight shouted with all his might.

"WAKE UP . . . WAKE UP . . . WAKE UP."

Gameknight awoke, surrounded by villagers. Crafter had a cold hand on his shoulders and was shaking him violently.

"I know how to wake him up," Hunter said. "I've done it before."

Sitting up, Gameknight pushed Crafter's hands off his shoulders, then held his hand up toward Hunter, stopping what he knew she was about to do.

"I'm awake . . . I'm awake!" Gameknight yelled.

"Are you alright?" Crafter asked.

Standing, Gameknight looked around the camp. He could see that everyone was awake, many with their weapons drawn. Digger stood near the perimeter, his big pickaxe held at the ready. Archers in the ice towers all had arrows drawn, ready for battle. The entire camp was like a coiled spring, compressed and ready to explode . . . all because of him. Looking to the east, he could see the sky start to brighten . . . it was dawn.

"We have to go," Gameknight said. "We have to hurry."

"What is it?" Hunter asked as she put away her bow and came up next to her friend. "What's going on?"

"I've seen Herobrine's plan and we can't delay," he said quickly. "We have to figure out how to defeat him before all those eggs hatch or we're doomed."

"Eggs? Have you finally lost you mind?" Hunter asked. "What are you talking about?"

"I'll explain later," he answered as he started to fold up his bed. "Right now we need to break camp and find that stronghold."

He could feel the puzzle pieces start to tumble around in his head. The secret to stopping Shaikulud and all those spiders was in there somewhere, but he couldn't see any of the pieces, the solution just a jumbled mess.

"We're in a race now against Herobrine and his spiders," he said as he turned to face Crafter, Digger now at his side, "and whoever comes in second place loses everything . . . including their lives."

CHAPTER 10

THE FATHER

The NPCs moved quickly across the frozen landscape. Gameknight was at the head of the column walking next to Digger. He ran when he could, walked when he couldn't, but drove the army of villagers as hard as he was able to. His feet were cold, his hands chilled to the bone, and his cheeks numb, but he didn't slow for an instant . . . too much was at stake.

They followed the narrow ravines that curved between the hills, still trying to stay out of sight while they followed the Eyes of Ender that Digger threw into the air every now and then. It was clear that the glowing orbs were leading them to the massive ice spike that was getting nearer; the Father. As they got closer, Gameknight could see that it was not a single thick ice spike, rather it was three glacial spires woven together in a complex pattern of overlapping and merging structures. It reminded him of how Mom used to braid Jenny's hair when she was younger, overlapping one strand with another until a thick rope formed. He couldn't imagine how this incredible structure could have naturally occurred, but Minecraft could do some amazing things sometimes.

Off to his right, Gameknight could see a thick spike of ice that was perhaps fifteen blocks high, its thick base made of snow. At the top of the frozen structure, he could see a section perhaps four blocks wide. Moving next to Crafter, he put a hand on the young NPC's shoulder.

"Crafter, do you still have any ender pearls from when we went to The End?" Gameknight asked.

"Let me look," the young NPC answered.

Ender pearls are what's dropped when an enderman is defeated. In their past adventures, Gameknight and his friends ventured to The End, the home of the endermen. There, with the Ender Dragon flying high overhead, they battled many of the shadowy monsters and collected many of the bluish pearls. As the main ingredient in the crafting recipe for making the Eyes of Ender, most of them had been consumed, but after searching his inventory, Crafter was able to pull out two of the blue spheres. Taking the pearls from Crafter's hands, Gameknight looked down at the glowing balls.

"What are you doing?" Monet asked.

"You can use ender pearls to teleport great distances, instantly," Gameknight explained. "I'm going up to the top of that spire and look around . . . make sure there aren't any monsters nearby."

"I want to go, too," she said.

Gameknight999 didn't answer. Turning, he moved to the base of the column of ice, then threw one of the ender pearls to the top of the frozen platform. Instantly, he was transported to where the sphere landed. Pain briefly erupted through his body as he took a little damage when he materialized, but he was still OK. Carefully looking across the icy landscape, Gameknight scanned the terrain for threats. When he saw nothing but blue ice and white snow, the User-that-is-not-a-user breathed a sigh of relief.

Taking the second ender pearl in his hand, he threw it back toward Monet. As he materialized next to his sister, he found Tiller approaching, a worried look on her face.

"You should be careful when you are doing these things," Tiller said, a motherly look of concern on her face.

"We're all clear," Gameknight999 yelled, then continued walking, Tiller and his sulking sister at his sides.

"Tiller, tell me about your daughter, Rider," Monet said. "What did she look like?"

Tiller smiled.

"She was the most beautiful NPC ever," she began. "Her hair was pure blond, as if spun from golden thread. It almost glowed when the red rays of sunset lit her face."

"She sounds beautiful," Monet added.

Tiller nodded.

"She was a lot like you, Monet. Rider had an independent spirit and did whatever she thought was right regardless of the consequences."

"I like her already," Monet said as she elbowed her brother in the ribs.

"Ouch," he said, then smiled.

"She loved riding the minecart tracks," Tiller continued. "Her job was to look for places where the minecart network was beginning to show through to the users. She was the best at finding these failures before they happened. Nobody questioned her judgment when she called for an abandoned mine to be constructed."

"That's right," Crafter added from ahead of them as he looked over his shoulder. "She had the best eye when it came to inspecting the rails."

Tiller smiled.

"How did she . . . die?" Monet asked.

"It was when Erebus, the King of the Endermen, attacked our village," Tiller said, her voice cracking with emotion. "She refused to stay back with the other women. Rider always said a woman could do anything that a man could do, and that also meant fighting to protect her village."

"She was right," Hunter shouted from behind.

Tiller looked back at Hunter and gave her a smile, then continued.

"When the zombies broke through the gates and charged into the village, she went running out with the men to stop the monsters . . . I never saw her again."

"Many people lost their lives that day," Crafter said.

Tiller nodded.

"Those first days of the war were terrible," Crafter added.

"But it's not over yet," Gameknight said. "There are still monsters out there that want to destroy us."

"And we want to destroy them as well," Hunter added.

Gameknight sighed, then reached past Monet and patted Tiller on the shoulder, his silent support the only thing he could offer her. She looked up at him and smiled, her warm hazel eyes filled with confidence in the User-that-is-not-a-user.

Ahead of them, Gameknight could see the massive ice spike, the Father, getting closer. As they neared, its tip disappeared into the clouds; the height of the structure unbelievable. When they came to its base, Digger threw another Eye of Ender. Instead of it flying off into the distance, it just stopped moving when it reached the Father, then fell straight to the ground.

"It's here," Digger said in a deep voice as he bent down to pick up the orb.

"OK, clear a space three blocks by three blocks in size," Gameknight instructed.

Digger pulled out his pick and knocked the snow off the nine blocks. Beneath them were more blocks of snow. Digging out the snow, he found dirt underneath. Once he had that finished, he looked up at the User-that-is-not-a-user.

"Now, build a spiral staircase going straight down."

"I though you weren't supposed to dig straight down?" Monet asked as she reached her brother.

"We aren't going straight down," Gameknight explained. "Digger is going to build a stairway that goes down one block then forward one block in a spiral pattern. The stairs will lead straight down, but will create safe steps." He then turned to Digger. "Start it now, and get anyone else you need."

"Digging is what I do," the big NPC replied with a smile. "I don't need any help."

"OK, the rest of you. We need fortifications around this spot. Hunter, you tell them what you want. I have the feeling that as soon as we enter the stronghold, Herobrine will know where we are."

"I'm on it," Hunter said, then spun and started giving commands, her curly red hair flinging about as she turned her gaze from here to there.

"What about me?" Monet asked.

"Not yet," Gameknight answered. "I need diggers. Anyone not building the fortifications, I want you to start mining. We need iron, just like before."

A dozen NPCs put away their swords and pulled out shovels. They chose a spot and all started digging, burrowing into the soil first with shovels and then with picks when they hit stone.

"What about me?" Monet whined.

"Not yet . . . I'll get to you."

Turning, he found Herder.

"Herder, I need your wolves out there sniffing around for monsters," Gameknight said. "I need the Wolfman to be ready. Here's what I want to you to do."

Gameknight explained his plan, sketching it out with the tip of his sword in the snow.

"I will do what you need," Herder said, a huge smile on his face.

He then put his fingers to his mouth and blew, making a loud shrill whistle. All of the wolves in the camp howled, then came running, following Herder as he headed away from the Father. After moving about ten blocks, half the pack headed to the north while Herder and the rest of the wolves headed to the south.

"Gameknight . . ." Monet said, her voice filled with frustration.

"Not yet!" he snapped. "Cavalry, I need mounted warriors."

Twenty warriors leapt onto their steeds and galloped to him.

"Guard the perimeter and watch for monsters . . . they'll be coming soon. If it is a small party of monsters, then destroy them." Gameknight looked at each NPC in the eyes as he gave the commands, knowing that these instructions would likely lead many of them to their deaths. "If it is a big party, then some of you have to stay and slow them down while the others get back to camp and warn the others."

Gameknight lowered his gaze, and his voice filled with sadness.

"I'm sorry that I have to ask this of you, but . . ."

"FOR MINECRAFT!" one of them yelled, then the others took up the battle cry as they road out.

"Gameknight . . . what can I do!" Monet asked, her voice now sounding desperate.

Turning, the User-that-is-not-a-user focused his gaze on the blacksmith and his apprentices.

"Smithy, I need you to place some of those arrow bombs out there in the open field," Gameknight explained. "That will probably be where the attack comes from."

The blacksmith nodded then ran off with his assistants, shovels in their hands.

"Gameknight . . ." Monet whined. "TOMMY!"

"Alright!" Gameknight snapped as he turned to face his sister.

"What do I do? I want to do something . . . I *need* to do something," she said. "This is my family now, too."

"Fine, here's what I want you to do," Gameknight explained. "You see that ice spire there." He pointed to the Father. "I want you and Stitcher to build steps up the side and find a good height from where you can see the surroundings. You are to then use Hunter's bow . . ."

"What?!" Hunter shouted.

"I said, Hunter *will* gladly give you her bow because she will be down in the stronghold with me and her bow won't be much use there." He glared at Hunter. She glared back, then smiled and handed Monet her enchanted bow. "Good, now, you and Stitcher are to watch for monsters, and when you see them, you are to shoot the arrow bombs. Do you understand?"

Monet smiled as she nodded her head.

"This is an important responsibility," Gameknight explained, "and dangerous. If you fall from up there . . ."

"I know, I'll 'hit the ground too hard,' right?" Monet said, reciting the message that Minecraft says when you fall . . . and die.

"Right," Gameknight answered, then moved closer to her and spoke in a low voice. "You don't have to do this, but it's just that we're kinda short of people and have a lot to do."

"I can do this . . . you can trust me," she said.

It sounded like something he would say to Dad when he was asking for responsibility, like when he'd been made responsible for his sister in his father's absence . . .

Why can't he be home!

He then thought about his friend in the physical world . . . Shawny.

SHAWNY . . . Is the digitizer working yet? he said in his mind, sending his thoughts out into the Minecraft servers, hoping his words would appear on his computer monitor.

Still dead, came the answer. *I'm taking apart some of the other contraptions in the basement, looking for some replacement components, but so far, I haven't found anything that can replace the fried parts.*

Keep at it, Gameknight thought to his friend. *We may need you real soon. Are there any users around?*

Everyone got disconnected but me, Shawny answered. *Some kind of shout or screech came through all the servers and kicked everyone off. Some of the Minecrafters thought they heard your name in the screech but no one is sure. All we know is that nobody can get to your server from outside of your house. I'm the only one here.*

Maybe you can send out the IP address using the forums and open up my dad's computer to them. Gameknight thought. *We might need some help before this thing is over.*

I'll be here, his friend replied.

Good!

He then turned to say something to the builders who were constructing the defenses when he heard Digger's booming voice echo from the curving stairway.

"I FOUND IT!" he shouted as he came running up out of the ground. "The stronghold . . . I reached the stronghold."

"Then it's time," Gameknight said. He turned and noticed that all the building and preparations had stopped, and all the NPCs were staring at him. "I'm going to only take a few of you with me down into the stronghold, but any of you can choose to stay up here and wait for our return." He paused to let his words sink in and to let the NPCs make their choices. "Any of you who are willing to go with me, and likely risk your life, raise your sword over your head."

Instantly, a hundred swords shot into the air, their razor sharp points gleaming in the sunlight. Even the children raised their wooden swords high over their heads, Topper and Filler, Digger's children, standing on their toes, trying to be noticed and selected.

Gameknight's heart swelled with pride. All of these NPCs were willing to face extreme danger. They could have chosen to stay on the surface and wait until they returned, but instead, they'd rather stand by his side and face the same danger that he was going to face.

Family truly does take care of family.

"OK, you and you and you . . ." Gameknight went through the camp and selected a handful of the best warriors, and headed for the stairway, Hunter, Digger, and of course Crafter close on his heels.

"Here we go," Gameknight said as he started down the steps.

Moving quickly, they descended downward, following the path Digger had carved into Minecraft. As they descended it grew cooler, the subterranean blocks sucking all the warmth and courage out of them. When they reached the bottom of the stairs, they found the pathway sealed by blocks of mossy cobblestone; it was the wall of the stronghold. Pulling out his pick, Gameknight broke the cobblestone. As soon as the block crumbled, a bat streaked out of the opening and headed up the curving stairway.

"Stop that bat . . . stop that bat!" Gameknight yelled.

But all the warriors, including Hunter, had their swords out. There was not a bow or arrow to be seen amongst them. And as the bat flitted up the staircase, Gameknight sighed. He looked at the NPCs who stood with him, and he knew that the die had been cast, and the real battle was about to begin.

How many of them will perish because of my mistakes . . . my failures? he thought. *I hate this responsibility. I just want to hide and be a kid again.*

But then a voice filled his mind. It was a voice not from within himself, but rather, it was from the very fabric of Minecraft.

You can accomplish only what you can imagine, the voice said.

Chills ran down his spine as the words echoed in his head for a moment, then disappeared.

Glancing around frantically, he looked at his friends.

"Did any of you hear that?" he said.

"Hear what?" Hunter replied. "You mean that squeaking bat . . . of course we all heard that."

"No, that voice," Gameknight said, a look of confusion on his face. "That strange voice . . . it was in my head."

"What did you say?" Crafter asked.

"I said I heard a voice," Gameknight asked.

"I always knew you were a little crazy," Hunter said. "But now you're creeping me out."

"Hunter!" Crafter snapped. "What did the voice say?"

"It said, 'You can accomplish only what you *can* imagine,' and then it disappeared."

"Wow . . . that sounds kinda smart," Hunter replied with a chuckle. "I wish I'd thought of it."

"Hunter, can't you ever be serious?" Crafter chided.

"Not if I can help it!"

"Enough! Time to focus," Digger said with his booming voice.

"Let's do this," Gameknight said, then stepped into the stronghold, fear nibbling at the edges of his courage.

CHAPTER 11
THE STRONGHOLD

A s soon as Gameknight999 stepped into the stronghold, he could sense the immense age of the place. It had a feel and smell of something that was ancient; it was likely a hundred years old if not older. Maybe it was part of the very first pre-alpha version . . . or maybe it was part of Notch's very first prototype. Gameknight wasn't sure, but he could certainly tell that this stronghold was different.

A long passageway stretched out to the left and right, the walls made of stone brick. Green moss could be seen encroaching along the walls as the sluggishly creeping lichen gradually invaded over the centuries. Running his hand across the cool blocks, Gameknight could feel that some of the bricks were cracked and worn with age. In the darkness, he could barely make out what was at the end of the hallway, though he could see the rough outline of something.

Placing a torch on the wall, Gameknight could see that the tunnel extended about twelve blocks in both directions, then reached a corner where the passageway turned. Iron bars were built into the stone walls and across the ceiling; likely they were supports to help hold up the ceiling. Moving to the metal support, Gameknight ran his blocky hand along the cold metal. The surface felt rough and pitted as rust had slowly eaten away at the bars over the years.

"OK, we need to find the library as quickly as possible," Gameknight explained. "I'm sure that Herobrine knows we're here. If not, then that bat will likely inform someone, so we don't have a lot of time. Crafter, any idea where we are?"

"We need to find the fountain room," the young NPC said. "Once we're there, then I think I can find the library."

Gameknight looked at the NPCs. There were twelve of them, counting himself. He wished there were more, but he didn't want to unnecessarily risk more lives.

"We should split up into groups of four and choose different passages to search," Gameknight said. "Plant torches behind you so that you know where you are going. Put them on the right side of the passage. When you've cleared a room, put torches on the left and right sides of the door. If you see a blank wall, break a few blocks to see if there is a hidden room on the other side. To get back here, follow the torches but have them on the left side. Hopefully no one will get lost. When anyone finds the library, yell and head back here. Everyone got it?"

They nodded, then went off in different directions.

Gameknight stayed with Hunter, Crafter, and Digger. They followed the passage to the right, then took a set of cobblestone stairs that led down to the next shadowy level. Right away, they found a chest sitting on a stone slab, blocks placed on either side of the wooden box. Moving carefully to check for traps, Gameknight cautiously opened the chest. The hinges creaked and groaned as the lid lifted, dust billowing into the air. Inside, he found some bread, an apple, and some iron ingots; he thought the iron might come in handy.

Collecting the contents, Gameknight closed the lid, then glanced down the passage and shuddered. Darkness shrouded the corridor. Placing a torch, light spilled outward, showing an empty brick hallway with iron bars embedded into cracked brick blocks and more mossy green blocks decorating the walls. Continuing on, they moved through the dim passages, carefully putting torches on the right wall.

Suddenly, a spider dropped down from the ceiling, landing right in front of Crafter. Before he could swing his sword, Digger hammered away at the monster with his pickaxe. Gameknight was shocked at the ferocity of his attack; the pick moved in a continuous blur, streaking at the monster too fast to be seen. The spider never had a chance.

"Thanks, Digger," Crafter said.

The big NPC smiled, then moved forward, checking the next passage.

A sorrowful moan drifted through the stone corridor, echoing off the walls and making it impossible to tell from which direction the wail originated.

"Zombies," Gameknight whispered. "We need to be careful."

Digger looked back at the User-that-is-not-a-user and nodded, then continued to lead the way, Hunter at his side, with Crafter placing the torches on the wall and Gameknight999 watching their rear. As they moved forward, they passed what Gameknight knew to be prison cells; the walls constructed with iron bars, the iron door standing open.

The zombie wail sounded louder; they were getting closer.

Gripping his sword firmly, Gameknight followed behind his friends, glancing frequently over his shoulder to make sure there were no monsters sneaking up on them. Ahead, he could see an iron door in the distance. The moans sounded as if they were coming from the other side. The party approached cautiously, weapons drawn but torches stored in their inventory; they didn't want to give away their presence.

Moving up to the door, Gameknight stood next to the iron button.

"Are all of you ready?" Gameknight whispered to his friends in the dark.

They all nodded.

"Crafter, you place a torch as soon as I open the door," Gameknight said. "We want to lure them into this room."

The young NPC nodded.

"Ready . . . now."

He hit the switch, causing the door to swing open. Instantly the hallway erupted with the moans and growls of zombies. Suddenly the room flared with light as Crafter planted his torch. Moving to face the door, Gameknight was shocked to see four villager-zombies, their pupils bright red. They swung their sharp black claws at him, but Hunter was too quick for them. Her iron sword tore into the monster, slowly whittling away at its HP. Gameknight turned to attack another creature, spinning to the left while his sword hit the monster's side. Stepping back, he let the creature come to him. Then he suddenly jumped into the air as he charged toward the monster, his sword swinging down onto the creature.

It disappeared with a *pop!*

Without waiting to see what it dropped, Gameknight turned to face the next beast; this one was charging toward Crafter. Its claws gleamed in the torchlight, making them appear to be glowing. Swinging low, he struck at the monster's legs while Crafter attacked up high. The zombie flashed red as their two swords sliced through the creature.

Pop . . . it disappeared.

A lone zombie now stood before them. Digger had it cornered, his big pickaxe ready to come down on the creature. Gameknight could see that its HP was almost depleted; a single hit would destroy the monster. Slowly, he approached.

"Where is the fountain room?" Gameknight asked.

The monster unconsciously glanced down the passage to the left.

Gameknight smiled.

The monster then looked up at the letters hovering over Gameknight's head, but then looked higher. The monster noticed the lack of a server thread, and realization of who Gameknight was came across the decaying face.

"The Maker searches for this . . . user," the zombie growled.

"I know that," Gameknight answered. "But the *Maker*, as you call him, is not going to find me."

"The Maker gave all zombies a message for the User-that-is-not-a-user," the creature said, his voice grumbling, almost like an animal.

Gameknight pitied this creature. He had at one time been a villager, but a zombie had infected him, and now he was this *thing* that stood before him. The NPC's mind had been changed from one that valued life to one that only wanted to destroy . . . it was sad.

"What is your message, zombie?" Hunter asked. "Tell us and we may let you live."

"The Maker told all zombies to destroy the NPCs of the Overworld until the User-that-is-not-a-user surrenders. Until that time, the zombies from all the servers will come to this server and punish those who claim the Overworld. The second great zombie invasion has begun and will only end with the surrender of the User-that-is-not-a-user."

The zombie looked at the NPCs, then back to Gameknight999.

"The message has been received?" the zombie asked.

"Yes, I heard your message!" Gameknight snapped.

The villager-zombie then almost looked contented, as if its suffering were about to be over. Growling, it then charged at Gameknight999, razor sharp claws extended. The three NPCs swung their weapons at the creature before it had even moved a single step. It disappeared with a *pop,* leaving behind some zombie flesh and three glowing balls of XP. Gameknight could have sworn that at the moment of the zombie-villager's death, he'd seen it smile.

"Quickly, this way," Crafter said as he bolted down the passageway to the left.

The others followed close behind as they moved through the dark corridors. Crafter placed torches as he went, Hunter and Digger at his side, Gameknight bringing up the rear. After about ten blocks, they reached a wooden door. Opening it carefully, they found a large, dark room, the sound of trickling water coming from the shadows. When Crafter placed a torch on the wall, the sight of a huge blue fountain greeted them. Water flowed out of a pedestal that had been placed exactly at the center of the room, the liquid falling into a recession that had been carved around the fountain.

"This is it," Crafter said as he looked about the room. "Hunter, Digger, both of you go back and bring the others. This is where our search really begins."

"This is where it begins?" Hunter asked. "What have we been doing all this time, just playing around?"

"Go now. Quickly," the young NPC said.

"Come on, Hunter," Digger said in his deep, booming voice. "We'll follow the torches back and find the others."

The two NPCs moved on, leaving Crafter and Gameknight999 alone.

Together, they moved about the room, placing torches and driving away the shadows. Clouds of dust swirled up into the air as their feet shuffled across the stone floor, making Gameknight want to sneeze. The sound of their feet echoed off the walls and came back to them from every direction, the only other sound being the trickling of water. It was clear that nobody had been in this room for a very, very long time. The lonely echoes of their feet made Gameknight feel as if they were completely alone, cut off from time and transported back to ancient days.

As they walked the perimeter of the chamber, the User-that-is-not-a-user suddenly thought he could hear some kind of sound . . . almost like a swishing-squeaking sound. He knew that he'd heard it before, but couldn't remember from where. It was a difficult sound to place with all the echoes and the trickling of water . . . impossible to recognize. But what he did know was the sound meant trouble, and it was somewhere down here in this stronghold . . . waiting for them.

CHAPTER 12

THE LIBRARY

In about five minutes, the sound of footsteps started to echo down the hallway and reach their ears. The other NPCs joined Gameknight and Crafter in the fountain room, led there by Digger, with Hunter bringing up the rear.

"Sorry it took so long," Digger said.

"We had to save some of these knuckleheads from a group of creepers," Hunter added.

"They had us trapped in a storage room," Planter said, lowering his head. "We didn't want to cause any to explode and set them all off . . . there were a lot of them."

"Didn't you ever hear about this new thing called fighting?" Hunter mocked. "I've told you a hundred times, when you see a creeper, you charge and don't let it finish its ignition. If you run away, you blow up."

"I know . . . we were a little scared."

Hunter moved to Planter's side and placed her hand on his shoulder.

"Next time, you'll do better, I'm sure," she said, her voice surprisingly free of sarcasm.

"We need to focus," Gameknight said. "Crafter, where is the library?"

"It's down one of these corridors," the young NPC said as he walked around the fountain.

The gurgling sound the water made masked the swishing that Gameknight thought he heard earlier.

"Then we split up and search them all," Gameknight said. "But we have to hurry."

They split up into groups of three, with Digger and Crafter staying with Gameknight, Hunter going with Planter and Carver. Baker and Weaver went with Stonecutter while Runner, Cobbler, and Carpenter took the last hallway. Each group took a passage and headed down a dark corridor, planting torches as they went.

Crafter took the lead for their group, Gameknight bringing up the rear. As they moved through the hallway, they heard the clicking of spiders and the clattering of bones, probably skeletons. Turning the corner, they came across a chest. Checking it for any traps, Digger opened it carefully. He found an iron sword and three apples.

"Keep the apples, Digger, you look hungry," Gameknight said.

"You take the sword, I have no use for it," Digger said has he slid his hand down the shaft of his pickaxe.

Suddenly, at the end of the darkened passage, an arrow streaked out of the shadows and bounced off Crafter's iron armor. Skeletons!

"Oh no you don't!" Gameknight yelled.

The User-that-is-not-a-user ran forward, ready to face the new threat. As he passed Digger, he pulled the iron sword from the big NPC's hand and held it with his left, his enchanted diamond sword in his right. Swinging both swords as if they were extensions of his own body, he tore into the skeletons with a rage. Attacking two monsters at the same time, he drove the enemy back against the wall. Slashing at one, Gameknight knocked the bow from the skeleton's bony hands. He then spun and sliced at another while deflecting a poorly shot arrow with his diamond sword. Leaping into the air, he swung at the monsters, tearing into their HP like a spinning tornado of destruction. In seconds, the hallway was littered with skeleton bones and balls of XP. He had destroyed them all.

Collecting the bones for Herder, Gameknight moved back to his friends. They both stared at him in shock and wonder.

"What was that?" Crafter asked.

"Well . . . I got a little mad that one of them shot at you."

"A little mad?" Digger asked. "You call that a little mad? I hate to see what furious looks like."

"And what was that with the two swords?" Crafter asked.

"I don't know," Gameknight answered. "It just felt like the right thing to do, I guess."

Crafter and Digger looked at each other in wonder, then turned back to stare at User-that-is-not-a-user.

"What?" Gameknight asked.

"The last person to wield two swords like that was my Great-Grandfather Smithy, during the first great zombie invasion," Crafter explained. "It rallied the NPCs to fight harder and changed the course of the war. It hasn't happened for a hundred years."

"Let's not make a big deal about this," Gameknight said. "Maybe we can just keep this to ourselves."

"Not a big deal?" Digger said.

"Keep it to ourselves?" Crafter added.

The two NPCs looked at each other, then laughed hard for the first time since . . .

"Come on," Gameknight said, his voice sounding frustrated, almost angry. "We need to find the library . . . we don't have time for this."

"Sometimes, User-that-is-not-a-user, it is important to notice those moments in your life that will change the course of everything," Crafter said.

"Whatever," Gameknight responded. "Let's get going."

"OK," Crafter acquiesced.

They continued following the hallway, checking all the rooms that branched off in different directions. No luck.

"Maybe we're in the wrong hallway," Digger said. "That would just be my luck."

"Wait . . . you smell that?" Crafter said as he drew in a big breath.

Gameknight and Digger stopped to inhale but sensed nothing.

"Follow me," the young NPC said as he ran off down the corridor.

The other two fought to keep up with Crafter as he sped forward, ignoring the dark shadowy corners.

Turning a corner, Gameknight found Crafter stopped before a wooden door. Light streamed out of the door's windows, filling the gloomy tunnel with a small bit of illumination. "It's here," Crafter said as he opened the door.

Instantly, the aroma of old dusty parchment wafted into the air. It smelled incredibly ancient, as if the age of the whole stronghold was compressed into this small library.

Gameknight stepped in and was greeted by shelves and shelves of books that stretched up over his head. He could see a second floor walkway that circled the room, bookshelves across every wall. An ornate chandelier hung at the center of the room, lighting both floors and driving the shadows from the sacred place.

Suddenly, there was movement to his left. A hissing sound filled his ears. Turning, he found a creeper just around the adjacent bookcase. Slashing at it with his diamond sword, he stopped its ignition and pushed it back a few steps. The creature just stood there and stared at him, its cold dead eyes filled with hatred and a desire to take his life. Well, it wouldn't get the chance. Charging at it, Gameknight hit the monster in the shoulder. It tried to ignite again, but Gameknight was already there, striking at it again and again, causing the ignition process to start over. In seconds, it was gone.

Then a zombie moan filled the room, then another. Heading toward the sound, Gameknight ran to the end of the bookcase and turned the corner, but then got stuck in some spiderweb, his sword and legs hopelessly entangled. Instantly, he was immobilized, unable to run and unable to lift his weapon . . . he was stuck. At the end of the aisle, he saw two zombies hiding in the few shadows that existed in the library. They saw him and charged forward, their dark razor sharp claws extended. As they shuffled forward, Gameknight struggled to free his sword. Pulling on the hilt, he tried to raise the weapon so that he could protect himself but it was no use. His arms only became more entangled in the sticky filament. He was caught.

The zombies came closer, their decaying stench starting to bite at his nostrils and turn his stomach.

I have to get my sword free . . . now!

He pulled with all his might, but the sticky web had its silky grip firmly around him.

They were getting closer.

He pulled with his free hand, hoping he could draw the iron sword and defend himself, but it too was stuck. He was starting to panic. Suddenly, a growling moaning sound came from behind him. Straining to look over his shoulder, he saw another zombie approaching from the opposite direction. He was surrounded.

The two zombies were almost on him.

He pulled harder and harder on the spiderwebs, but they did not yield.

Should I yell out for help? he thought. *But it might attract more monsters.*

Looking at the approaching monsters, he could see they were only a few steps away . . . he had no choice. But just as he was about to yell, Digger turned the corner and sprinted toward the two creatures.

"I don't think so!" he yelled, his booming voice echoing throughout the library, causing dust to fall from the shelves. "FOR MINECRAFT!"

His pickaxe was a blur as it tore into the two creatures. The monsters turned when they felt the bite of his mighty pick and reached out with their dark claws, but they stood little chance. Digger smashed into one, then chopped at the other, tearing the HP from them in seconds.

And suddenly, where there used to be two monsters, there were none.

A moan sounded behind Gameknight. Turning his head, he could see the last zombie was almost on him. Digger was at the other end of the aisle, too far away to help. Gameknight tugged and tugged at his sword arm, but it was still stuck.

"Gameknight, don't move!" Digger yelled.

"Don't move? Are you kidding? I *can't* move!"

"Good!" the big NPC replied.

Holding the end of the pick's handle with two hands, he brought it high up over his head, then stepped forward and threw it with all his might. The tool spun through the air, end-over-end, until it hit the zombie with a *thunk.* The creature stumbled around, flashing red again and again. And then Crafter was at its back, slashing at the creature with his own blade. In seconds, it was gone.

Stepping up to Gameknight999, Crafter chopped at the spiderweb with his sword—the only way to efficiently cut through the silky strands.

"Are you OK?" Crafter asked.

"Yeah . . . thanks to Digger, and you."

"I found what we're looking for," Crafter said. "Come quick."

The young NPC ran to a ladder that led to the top floor, the others following close behind. Then, dashing around the raised walkway, he stopped in front of one bookshelf, the tomes before him looking ancient and worn. Gameknight could see what looked like the same books they'd seen in the last stronghold, before going to The End. He saw numerous titles that he recognized: a book called *The Great Zombie Invasion,* another called *The Great Shame of the Ghasts,* one called *The Joining,* and one that looked older than all the rest. It was called *The Awakening.*

How is it that these books are here, when I saw them in the other stronghold library on a totally different server?

He reached out and pulled down *The Awakening*, looking at the cover with wonder and confusion in his eyes.

"I know what you are thinking," Crafter said. "How is it that these books are here, when we saw them in the other library?"

Gameknight nodded.

"You see, stronghold libraries are like ender chests," Crafter explained. "What goes into one stronghold library goes into all of them. Every library has all the same books, no matter which server someone is on."

Gameknight nodded again as he put the ancient book back on the shelf. Crafter then reached in front of Gameknight and pulled down a volume called *The Oracle*.

"Here's what I was looking for," Crafter said.

"Maybe we should just take it and go?" Gameknight asked.

Crafter shook his head.

"These books can never leave the library," Crafter explained. "If they do, then they will turn to dust. They can only survive the ravages of time within these walls. We must read it here."

"Then Digger, go get the others and bring them here," Gameknight commanded. "Follow the torches back to the fountain room."

"Consider it done," Digger said as he sprinted back toward the ladder and disappeared from sight.

"OK, let's find the information we need and get out of here," Gameknight said to his friend. "I have the feeling that something really bad is about to happen."

"This will be quick," Crafter said has he shuffled quickly through the pages. "Here it is . . . ahh . . . this is what we need. It says, 'The Oracle is a creature of power and wonder. She was brought into Minecraft to save us from the ravages on the Intruder. Though her solution is not quick, it will save us all, in the end. It will take the strength and sacrifice of many to stop the Intruder, but all hope rests on the User-that-is-not-a-user. Only he can save Minecraft from this threat. It will seem impossible, at times, for the Intruder is strong and resourceful, but the User-that-is-not-a-user must not give up. You can accomplish only what you can imagine.' It goes on for a while here, and . . ."

"What did it say at the end there . . . the last sentence?" Gameknight asked.

"Ahh . . . oh, here it is . . . 'You can accomplish only what you can imagine.' That's what that voice said to you, right?" Crafter asked. "It was as if the text was talking directly to you."

Gameknight shivered for just an instant, then looked up at Crafter.

"Does it say how to find the Oracle?" Gameknight asked.

Crafter shuffled through more of the book, then stopped on a page that was slightly torn. It looked as if there were stains on the page, like something had been spilled across the bottom . . . something red.

"It says, 'Continue the path set forth by the great spires of ice. The two juniors point to the senior, which points the way to the Oracle. Follow the rising sun and you will find her temple. But beware of the jungle, for it hides deadly creatures that will stop all but the most brave and resilient.'"

Crafter closed the book and put it back on the shelf. As he turned to face Gameknight999, he heard a commotion on the ground floor of the library, many feet shuffling across the dusty wooden floor. Drawing his diamond sword, Gameknight moved to the ladder and held his sword up high, ready to attack. Hunter's red hair suddenly popped up through the opening, her warm brown eyes staring up at him.

"You looking to give me a hair cut or something?" she said with a smile. "Nothing personal, but I don't think so." She then glanced at Crafter. "You find what you need?"

The young NPC nodded his head and smiled.

"Then let's get out of here," she added as she dropped back down the ladder.

Gameknight followed her down the ladder and found a collection of NPCs in the library, some of them out in the stone hallway. Digger stood next to the door, his mighty pickaxe resting on his shoulder.

"We have what we need," Gameknight said to the NPCs.

Glancing at the collection, he could see that some were missing.

"Where are Planter and Baker and Weaver?" Gameknight asked.

"They're guarding the tunnel," Digger answered. "We thought it best to . . ."

Suddenly a voice echoed down the stone passage.

"CREEPERS!" the voice yelled. It was Planter. "CREEPERS!"

An explosion shook the very foundation of the stronghold, the blast cutting off Planter's voice abruptly. A cloud of dust billowed down the hallway, making the NPCs cough and struggle for breath.

A scream pierced through dusty air, followed by a sound that could only have been a stone block being broken. Another explosion rocked the hallway, followed by the sounds of more broken blocks.

"What's going on?" Baker asked, his voice shaking with fear.

"I don't know," Digger answered, "but I think we should get out of here."

"I agree," Gameknight said. "Let's get going."

As he stepped out into the hallway, his ears were instantly filled with that swishing-squeaking sound, like some kind of creature scurrying across the floor. But this time it didn't sound as if it were just a lone creature; this time it sound like there were many.

Turning to look at his companions, he could see that they all heard the sound . . . and they all looked scared.

"What is that sound?" Carver asked.

"I don't know," answered Runner.

"I know what it is," Gameknight answered, his voice filled with trepidation and fear.

"What?" Hunter asked. "What is it?"

"It's the swarm."

CHAPTER 13

THE SWARM

They ran out of the library and headed toward the only exit they knew. The problem was that they were also running toward that swishing-squeaking sound. Turning the corner, they found a section of the passageway completely missing, chunks of floor and wall that were clearly victim to the creepers' explosive embrace. Torches lay scattered on the ground as well as some inventory items . . . likely the remains of the missing NPCs.

Suddenly, they heard feet running toward them through the darkness. Drawing his sword, Gameknight moved to the front of the group and readied himself for battle. Hunter moved next to him and placed a torch on the wall. As the circle of light expanded, they saw Weaver running straight toward them, a look of panic on his face. His iron armor was dented and cracked as if he'd been in a huge battle.

"They're coming! Run!" Weaver said as he approached.

He reached Gameknight and Hunter, but did not stop. Digger reached out and grabbed the NPC and held him tight, but the villager's momentum knocked both of them to the floor.

"Weaver," Crafter said as he helped the NPC to his feet, "try to calm down and tell us what happened."

"They're both gone," he said as he was trying to catch his breath. "They were both standing there, then Planter saw the creepers and charged them. He got two of them before the others exploded."

"Are all the creepers gone?" Hunter asked.

"Only one survived, but that one got Baker," Weaver said.

"So they're all gone," Hunter said. "We're OK?"

"NO!" Weaver snapped. "There was something there other than the creepers!" He paused for a moment to catch his breath, then continued. "They came out of the blocks . . . little spiny things with segmented bodies."

Hunter looked at Gameknight as if she didn't believe what she was hearing.

"I saw them!" Weaver added. "They were the color of stone . . . all gray. At first we didn't see them; the little monsters blended in with the stone brick, but then we saw their tiny eyes reflecting the light of the torches. We thought they might be bats, but then they started making that weird swishing sound. Suddenly, they were all around us, coming right out of the blocks. I killed a couple, but for every one I hit, another jumped out of a block, and then another and another."

"What are you talking about?" Crafter asked him.

"Silverfish," Gameknight said, the swishing-squeaking sound suddenly making sense to him. "They're throughout the strongholds. You kill one and two more come out of the blocks. That's what we heard swishing and squeaking back near the fountain room. Silverfish must have been the swarm that got all the kids way back when."

"What do we do?" Carver asked. "Fight?"

"NO!" Gameknight snapped. "We don't fight, we run. Silverfish never stop attacking, and when you wound one, it calls out to the others hiding nearby in the blocks, increasing their number until they swarm over everything in their path." Gameknight gazed at his comrades, making sure they were all listening, for all their lives depended on this. "No, we don't fight . . . we run, as fast as we can."

Just then, the passageway filled with the swishing-squeaking sounds of a large group of silverfish. They all turned and faced the sound. From the darkness, Gameknight could see beady eyes staring at them. And then one of them stepped into the light. It was grayish in color and had a rat-like body that was segmented with tiny armored plates. Needle sharp spines stuck out along their back and tail, making them deadly to touch. Gameknight cringed at the sight of them.

What was Notch thinking when he added these to the game?

"We can't just stand here," Stonecutter said. "We have to do something."

"We're going to do something," Gameknight added. "We're going to run." He then turned and faced the other NPCs. "Don't stop for anything. If you stop to fight, the monsters will surround you and quickly you'll be overwhelmed. Run . . . and run for your lives."

Putting his sword away, Gameknight turned to face the disgusting little creatures, then sprinted right at them, his eyes on the exit corridor that lay on the other side of the swarm. He could hear the others behind him following, but he didn't dare turn back and look.

As soon as he neared the silverfish, he jumped over it, then jumped sideways as another shot toward him. He turned the next corner and found the hallway filled with at least twenty of the creatures, waiting for him. Resisting the urge to draw his sword, he ran straight for the monsters, jumping as high as he could. But behind him, he heard the sound of tiny little squeals as one of the NPCs stabbed at the monsters with their sword.

"NO, DON'T ATTACK THEM!" he shouted, but his voice was drowned out by the echoes of swords glancing off stone.

CRACK!

He heard a block break nearby. Two more creatures leapt toward him. Dodging to the side, he continued his run. But as he sprinted, he heard more blocks breaking, the volume of the swishing-squeaking getting louder and louder.

A scream pierced through the tunnel as one of the NPCs fell. He could tell by the sound that silverfish were overwhelming the poor soul. Resisting the urge to go back and help, Gameknight knew that all he could do right now for his friends was get to the exit and make sure it was secure.

Following the torches, he wove his way through the twisting tunnels, shooting up flights of steps and down deserted hallways. Everywhere, he saw silverfish popping out of blocks and the foolish NPCs behind him tried to fight them off. Jumping over what he thought was the last of the little monsters, he streaked toward Digger's spiral staircase. More screams echoed from behind him, but he kept running. He could hear their footsteps close behind. The silverfish were now behind the party and were chasing down the slowest of the group.

Another scream echoed through the hallway as the sound of an iron sword ringing off stone filled his ears. Whoever was back there was trying to fight them off, but with every blow he landed, two more silverfish popped out of the walls. And then the screams stopped as the sword clattered to the ground.

Another one gone because of me.

And then they were at the stairs. Gameknight stopped to place more torches, raising the light level so that they could all see better.

"Go, up the stairs!" Gameknight yelled as he stood by the exit.

Carver, who was right behind him, shot up the stairs without a word, followed by Runner and Cobbler. Hunter reached his side and pushed him toward the exit.

"Go!" she shouted.

But Gameknight shook his head.

"Not until the others are safe," he replied. "You go!"

"I'll wait here for a while," she said as she drew her sword.

The sounds of scraping tails mixed with the scurrying of tiny little feet filled the corridor.

"Here come the others," Hunter said as she moved forward, her sword held low.

Gameknight could see Crafter and Digger running with all their might, Carpenter bringing up the rear. Suddenly, Carpenter fell. His screams filled the passage as a wave of scaly silverfish flowed over him like an ocean wave. His body flashed red over and over like a blinking strobe . . . and in seconds he was gone.

"NOOOO!" Gameknight yelled.

"Get up the stairs!" Crafter yelled as he ran. "I have an idea how to slow them down and keep them in the stronghold."

Hunter turned and ran up the stairs while Gameknight stood there waiting for his friends. Digger shot past him without even slowing down, leaving Gameknight and Crafter to face the multitudes.

"What are you going to do?" Gameknight asked.

"Soul sand," Crafter said as he backed toward the stairs. "Silverfish can't cross soul sand without taking damage." He placed a couple of blocks on the ground in front of him. "It just came to me while I was running. I still had some blocks in my inventory from the last time we went to the Nether. You still remember that?"

He smiled as he placed more blocks of the brown sandy cubes. Backing up farther, he continued to place the blocks before them, forming an unbroken line. A few of the creatures tried to get over the blocks, but they flashed red as soon as they touched them. One of the silverfish was fast enough to get over the soul sand, but Gameknight struck at it as soon as it was close. It disappeared with a puff, but was joined by the sound of breaking blocks; more silverfish had spawned.

"Get up the stairs," Crafter said. "I've got this."

Turning, Gameknight shot up the stairs as Crafter followed, placing blocks of soul sand as he climbed. Gameknight's fear slowly eased as the light of day filtered down the rocky steps and brightened the walls with a golden hue. But when he exited the stairway and finally saw the blue sky overhead, he was greeted with the sounds of chaos.

NPCs were running everywhere, many of them yelling and in a panic.

"What is it?" Gameknight asked as Teacher ran by.

"Monsters heading this way," she said as she donned her armor and drew her sword. "They're out on the open plain just as you predicted."

Without waiting for any response, she turned and headed for her spot on the defensive wall, moving between a woodcutter and the blacksmith.

Looking about the landscape, he could see NPCs all taking up arms and positioning themselves behind walls or in towers, ready to stand up against the approaching wave of violence.

An eerie silence settled across the camp. Gameknight could feel a cold wind blowing across the biome. The gentle breeze pushed and pulled on the tall glacial spikes, making some of them vibrate like tuning forks, adding a harmonious humming sound to the scene. For the briefest of moments, it was beautiful . . . until the wind shifted and the sound of clicking spiders and zombie growls filled the air. Looking up to the Father, he could see Monet and Stitcher at the ready, their faces lit with an iridescent hue from their magical bows. Monet waved down at him, then pointed out toward the oncoming horde. Gameknight moved up a nearby hill of snow and looked across the icy plain. He could see a large group of spiders approaching, their fuzzy black bodies standing out in stark contrast against the snow-covered ground. Intermingled amongst the eight-legged monsters were zombies and skeletons, all wearing leather hats, some wearing armor. He guessed there were maybe sixty total in the mob; not the most they'd had to face on this journey, but still a sizeable force. Looking down on the villagers, he knew that many would not leave this place, and this thought made him sad. Hopefully the plans they'd laid would help stem the tide of destruction and protect as many of his friends . . . no, his family . . . as possible.

"Crafter!" he yelled down the hill. "Send up the first rocket."

The young NPC had a huge smile on his face as he planted a small red and white striped object on the ground. As soon as he released it, the rocket shot high up into the air, then exploded, forming a gigantic sphere of glistening orange sparks that danced around like fireflies. That was the signal for everyone to get ready, especially for those hidden from view.

Running down the hill, Gameknight found Crafter and pulled on his sleeve.

"Iron . . . how much iron did the miners get?" he asked.

"Only enough for two," Crafter answered.

"Fine, get them ready," Gameknight explained, "but don't complete their construction until I give the word."

Crafter nodded as he pulled out blocks of iron and started stacking them into the shape of a T, then placed two pumpkins on the ground nearby.

The clicking grew louder, and Gameknight could see the look of fear on many of the NPCs' faces.

"Hold your ground!" he shouted to all of them. "We're here to defend Minecraft and everyone that lives on all the servers. We won't let these monsters take that from us!"

The NPCs cheered.

Looking to the second defensive wall, he could see Tiller in her dented iron armor, her sword gripped firmly in her hand. She gave him a warm motherly smile that filled him with guilt.

I hope this is going to work, Gameknight thought. *I can't bear to be responsible for even one more death.*

And then the mystical words that he'd heard down in the stronghold echoed through his mind again.

You can accomplish only what you can imagine.

He didn't understand what it really meant. Gameknight999 knew that this was somehow important, but he couldn't figure it out.

Accomplish what you can imagine? he thought to himself.

He still didn't get it, but maybe the villagers would.

"Be strong friends," he yelled. "We can do this . . . I can feel it, and you should too." He then walked up to the swordsmen who stood at the first wall—these would likely be the first to lose their lives. That's where he would stand . . . with them. "We will swat this mob aside as if it were made of annoying insects. They will feel the sting of our swords and arrows, and go back to Herobrine with their tails between their legs!"

The warriors laughed and cheered as the image of the defeated army retreating back to their masters filled their minds. But then the laughter stopped as the monsters moved into view.

The horde covered the plain before them, the mass of bodies all crowded together. Gameknight looked up at Monet and Stitcher and hoped that they would not miss.

The monsters came closer. They could now hear the zombies growling and moaning, their stench wafting on the gentle breeze and assaulting their senses.

Gameknight raised his hand, signaling the two archers to get ready.

One of the skeletons launched an arrow at the front rank of NPCs, but the shaft missed its target and stuck in the snow-covered ground.

Almost there, he thought, *just a little closer.*

The warriors started to yell at the monsters, casting insults as if they were projectiles. The monsters growled back. Gameknight could see a look of utter hatred in their eyes and knew that this would be a fight to the death; none of these monsters would surrender.

The creatures passed the blocks of snow that had been carefully placed on the battlefield, none of the monsters looking to see what was hidden behind the frozen cubes.

"NOW!" Gameknight yelled.

Stitcher and Monet both fired their flaming arrows at the hidden arrow bombs. Stitcher's hit its target on the first shot, but Monet's missed and stuck into a zombie instead. The green monster burst into flames and started running around, then fell over and disappeared. Firing another arrow, she hit her mark on the second, the black and red cubes instantly starting to blink.

The first arrow bomb went off, throwing a hundred arrows into the air. Then the second one exploded, adding another group of projectiles to the deadly rain. Not watching what was about to happen, Gameknight turned and signaled to Crafter. The young NPC placed the pumpkins on top of the stacks of iron blocks, and instantly, two iron golems came to life. Looking at the collection of monsters, the iron giants instantly headed toward their enemies.

Signaling Crafter again, the young NPC fired another rocket into the air. This one exploded high overhead, showing the face of a sparkling green creeper—it was the signal to the cavalry.

"Archers, open fire," Gameknight yelled, then turned to the warriors on the first defensive wall. "All of you stay here and keep the monsters from advancing. Hold this wall, but don't take any unnecessary risks . . . got it?"

They all nodded back to their leader.

Screams of pain echoed from the monster horde as the arrows fell down upon them, rending HP from monster bodies. Gameknight turned and watched, but could see that some of the spiders had moved forward, out of the deadly rain. They were charging toward the defenders on the wall.

Suddenly, Gameknight999 was filled with an uncontrollable rage.

You aren't going to hurt my family!

"OH NO YOU WON'T!" he yelled.

Drawing his iron and diamond swords, the User-that-is-not-a-user leapt over the wall and charged at the spiders, attacking the lead spider with both blades. It disappeared quickly. Turning, he attacked the next one with his diamond blade while he was swiping at another with his iron sword. Spinning to the side, he struck at another monster while blocking razor sharp claws. Jumping and leaping, he was impossible to hit as he hacked at one monster after another. Then suddenly there was a warrior at his side . . . then another and another, a flash of black and gray showing out of the corner of his eye. Not bothering to look who it was, Gameknight pressed the attack, tearing at the spiders, refusing to let them advance any further.

The ground shook with thunder as the cavalry arrived, smashing into the back of the monster formation. Fifty NPCs attacked on horseback, some with swords, some with bows. The large horses, with their heavy armor, pushed through the horde as if wading through a violent river. Their hooves became weapons as they also joined the fray.

Then the iron golems reached the battle lines. The mighty giants swung their arms through the mass of monsters, throwing spiders and zombies high into the air, their bodies flashing red. Stepping back, Gameknight signaled to Crafter one last time. Another rocket soared into the air and exploded, forming a sparkling orange and blue star.

Howling filled the air as Herder and his wolves sped forward. The monsters heard the noise and a look of fear covered their hideous faces, but they had no place to go. They were surrounded by warriors at the front, cavalry at the back, and iron golem in their midst. Gameknight could hear arrows whistling past his head from the archers up in the towers, but they stopped their barrage when the wolves arrived, the furry white animals leaping at the monsters with lethal efficiency.

In minutes, it was over. Not a single monster survived. Looking at the scattering of items across the ground, Gameknight noticed an absence of armor, swords, and bows.

Could it be? he thought.

And then he heard Crafter's voice shouting out.

"We've defeated the monster horde without losing a single person!"

The NPCs cheered and shouted, their weapons held high in the air.

"Hail the User-that-is-not-a-user, wielder of the two-swords!" Digger shouted with his deep voice.

The NPCs cheered again, but Gameknight raised his hands to silence his friends.

Suddenly, a scream pierced through the cheering crowd.

It was Monet113.

Turning to look at her, Gameknight could see her streaking down the last steps that hugged the Father, then sprinted across the battlefield to someone in dented iron armor who was lying on the ground.

Oh no . . .

Running to the fallen NPC, he reached her at the same time as his sister.

Falling to her knees, Monet carefully pulled off her iron helmet to expose the salt-and-pepper hair, a pair of hazel eyes staring up at her in agony. Gameknight knelt to her side and could see that her armor was battle damaged, deep tears in it from spider claws. Huge chunks of metal were missing where the monsters had attacked her. He could tell that her HP was nearly exhausted . . . she would not survive.

Tiller looked up at Gameknight999.

"You should be . . . careful out there on . . . the battlefield, dear," she struggled to say to him. "There were a . . . lot of monsters around you. I couldn't . . . couldn't leave you . . . there alone."

It was you *at my side,* he thought.

As his memory played it back, he realized that Tiller had rushed to his side, causing all the other warriors to charge forward. She was a hero.

"Tiller, you should have stayed where it was safe," Monet said. "You're hurt, but I'm sure you'll be alright . . . right?" She looked up at Crafter.

The young NPC just shook his head.

"I couldn't stand there . . . and watch your . . . brother fight all . . . alone," Tiller said between coughs. "I did that when . . . Rider went out to . . . fight on that terrible day. I couldn't do that again."

The woman was raked by a series of violent coughs. Once they stopped, she looked up at Gameknight, then Monet. Reaching out, she took Gameknight's hand, then took Monet's.

"You two are . . . brother and sister. Rely on each other, for there is . . . no bond like that held by siblings. You have to . . . support each other no matter what. Gameknight, trust your . . . sister. Monet, listen to your brother. You are both in this together, and when it comes time to face impossible . . . odds, you will only have each other. Remember . . ."

And then Tiller disappeared as the last of her HP evaporated, causing her armor to just fall to the ground and float as if riding on unseen waves.

An anguished wail came from Monet1113 as she yelled and screamed and cried, overcome with grief. Gameknight stood up and lifted his sister, then wrapped his arms around her, holding her tight. The two of them stood there, holding onto each other for strength as they both cried. And then a pair of arms wrapped around them. Stitcher enveloped the pair of them with her short arms and held on tight, supporting them with all her strength. Another pair wrapped around the brother and sister; Crafter lending his own support. The supportive arms of the entire village of NPCs stepped forward to hug some of the pain away from the pair; the family taking care of its own. And as one, the entire village wept.

Finally Gameknight released his sister. Slowly, he raised his hand high over his head, fingers held out wide, he spoke to everyone.

"Let us not forget Tiller, the only casualty of this battle, and those who we lost down in the stronghold," Gameknight said solemnly. "Good friends and family will be remembered for their sacrifice on this day."

Slowly, he squeezed his hand into a fist, clenching it tighter and tighter until he could hear his knuckles crack and pop. Every bit of anger and rage was held within that fist, and he squeezed it with all his might. Gameknight then slowly lowered his hand as he bowed his head for a moment, then raised his head and looked about the camp.

Suddenly, the ground shook as the two iron golems approached. The two metal giants stopped in front of Gameknight999 and looked down at him, their dark eyes looking at him with sympathy and respect.

"Thank you for your help," Gameknight said to the pair. "You did well protecting these villagers from the monsters of Minecraft . . . you should be proud."

The metal giants smiled.

"But there is one more thing that you could do to help protect the NPCs," Gameknight explained. "Go to the king of the golems and tell him what is happening. He knows me and knows that I would not ask for his help if it were not necessary, but I feel that we will need the help of the golems before this war is over. Tell him that I will give a signal, somehow, and that he should send all his golems, for the very survival of Minecraft may depend on his haste. Do you understand?"

The golems nodded, then turned and lumbered across the icy landscape, heading for their home and their king.

Gamekight999 then turned and faced the other NPCs.

"Break camp," the User-that-is-not-a-user commanded as he wiped tears from his eyes. "Herobrine will send more monsters after us, as this was just the smallest taste of his wrath. We are still in a race for our lives and all the lives in Minecraft. Today we won a battle, but the war still rages on." He paused as he turned and looked across the battlefield at all the NPCs. "Everyone get ready . . . we head to the Oracle in the Jungle Temple."

CHAPTER 14

HATCHLINGS

Shaikulud moved about the chamber, checking on her precious eggs. Some were starting to hatch, but very few. She could see the baby spiders gorging themselves on the green moss the Brothers had been retrieving from the dungeons and could almost see them bulge outward and get bigger while she watched. The green moss made the young hatchlings grow faster than any other plant life; it was their favorite.

Moving toward the entrance, the spider queen had a yearning to warm herself in the sun. She wanted to climb up on the top of the tall jungle-wood tree and bathe in the warming rays of the sun, but she couldn't leave the nest . . . not right now.

Sighing, she moved to the side of the cavern and started climbing up the wall. Before she could make it half way up, a bat flitted into the cave and headed straight for her. Seeing it, she dropped to the ground and waited for the little messenger. The dark bat moved erratically through the cave; why they couldn't fly in a straight line was a mystery.

Flying a zigzag course, the shadowy creature finally landed on her front leg. Moving close to the spider queen's head, the bat whispered his message. Shaikulud gasped in surprise.

Suddenly, there was a presence next her. It was an evil presence, boiling over with hatred and spite. Turning her head, she saw Herobrine standing before her, his appearance again changed to that of a new NPC, his latest victim.

"What news is there, Shaikulud?" Herobrine asked.

"Thissss bat tellsssss me that the User-that-is-not-a-user hassss been spotted."

"Where?" he snapped.

"He wassss seen going into the stronghold," she replied.

"The stronghold?!" he snapped. "They must be looking for the library."

"Some of the Sisterssss went out to meet him in battle, but they were few in number." She paused to toss the bat into the air. It flitted about, then flew to the cavern opening. "It issss unlikely that they were able to vanquish the NPCssss."

"It is of no concern," Herobrine said as he paced back and forth.

Pondering this news, his eyes grew brighter and brighter until their evil radiance nearly lit the whole chamber. Shaikulud had to look away so as not to be blinded.

"Very good," he said, his eyes starting to slowly dim back to their normal evil level. "Everything is proceeding as I have foreseen." He then cackled an evil knowing laugh that echoed through the chamber.

"What are your instructionsssss, Maker?" Shaikulud asked as she bowed her head.

Herobrine looked about the chamber at all the eggs that were yet to hatch, and a guttural growl came from his throat. He then moved to the nearest one.

"I thought the hatchlings would be here by now," he grumbled.

"Not yet," Shaikulud answered as she followed her master.

"They have to be ready now!" he snapped. "Open the eggs and bring forth the hatchlings. I will have use of them very soon." He then spun and glared directly into Shaikulud's multiple purple eyes. "That's an order!"

"But opening them too soon may damage the hatchlingssss," Shaikulud said in her meekest voice. "Would it not be better to wait until the eggssss are ready?"

"The User-that-is-not-a-user marches on you right now. His only intent is to destroy all of your children. Are you going to let that happen?" Herobrine glared at Shaikulud, his eyes glowing brighter. "Because of this Gameknight999, they must be hatched NOW!"

Herobrine's shout echoed off the walls of the cavern and made the many bats hanging on the ceiling scatter for cover.

"I will ask one more time," he continued as he moved closer to the spider queen. This time his voice was at a dangerously low volume, one that only Shaikulud could hear. "Do you understand me?" he growled.

"I understand the Maker . . . and will follow hissss commandssss," she replied.

"Excellent," he replied as his eyes dimmed. "You will allow the User-that-is-not-a-user and his friends to reach the old hag's temple. Do not stop them. Let them through, but take the opportunity to make them suffer a bit so that it doesn't seem too easy. Use the creepers; they will be hard to see in the jungle.

"When they reach the temple, with their backs against the sea, we will close the trap and surround them. You will then signal the attack and leave none alive except for Gameknight999. If the hag is brave enough to venture outside of her temple, then destroy her as well. We will destroy them all with the same stroke. And when this pathetic User-that-is-not-a-user is mad with grief, then I will confront him and teach him what true suffering really is.

"Do you understand your instructions . . . all of them?"

Shaikulud bowed her head again.

"It will be done," she said as she stared at his feet.

"Very good," Herobrine said in a menacing tone. "I always knew you were good and obedient."

As she raised her head to look up at Herobrine, he teleported away, his glowing eyes the last thing to disappear. She then turned and faced the spiders that were now moving toward her.

"You heard the Maker," she said, her mandibles clicking together angrily. "Open the eggssss and release the hatchlingssss."

The blue cave spiders looked at her in disbelief, then glanced at each other. Shaikulud then moved with a speed that anyone would have thought impossible for a creature as large as her. She raked at the nearest cave spider with her razor sharp claws, tearing into the Brother's HP until it was nearly exhausted. It happened so fast, the cave spider didn't even have a chance to run away.

Falling to the ground, the cave spider looked up at his queen with its multiple red eyes pleading for mercy.

Stepping back, Shaikulud turned and glared at the other spiders in the chamber.

"You will follow the instructionssss of the Maker . . . open the eggssss."

The wounded cave spider slowly climbed back to his feet and moved to the nearest egg. With his front claw, he carefully carved a narrow scratch into the outer surface of the egg. After going all the way around, he tapped at it along the scratch, causing a crack to form. In seconds, the top half of the egg was removed, showing an extremely small spider within. It was another cave spider, its blue skin almost glowing fluorescent due to the lack of the tiny black hairs that would come in later . . . if it survived.

"Give it moss, quick," Shaikulud commanded.

Another Brother came forward with a clump of moss, but the tiny spider died before it could feed.

My hatchling . . . my hatchling . . .

Shaikulud mourned the loss of the tiny creature, but continued to oversee the opening of the eggs.

"It issss the Maker'ssss will," she said over and over.

Many of the hatchlings survived this premature emergence into Minecraft, but still many died. And as her hatchlings disappeared with a *pop,* her anger grew . . . not toward Herobrine, for she knew that he was doing what he must to protect Minecraft. No, her anger was focused on the one responsible for her loss . . . the User-that-is-not-a-user.

As she picked up one hatchling that was struggling to survive, she thought of all the ways she wanted to make this Gameknight999 suffer. Suddenly, the hatchling disappeared as its HP gave out and her rage boiled over.

"The User-that-is-not-a-user is MINE!" she shouted to all the spiders in the cavern, her eyes glowing bright purple. "No one is to harm him but me! I alone get to make him suffer."

As the echoes of her voice reverberated through the cavern, Shaikulud moved to the cavern wall and climbed up its vertical surface. Moving across the arching ceiling, she could feel all the new lives emerging from the eggs below, some only lasting a fleeting instant. When she reached the top of the cavern's roof, her razor sharp claws dug into the stone and held her fast as she watched the life and death scenes play out on the floor below. For every new life, she could feel a drain on her mind as another slice of her awareness was used to hold that new spider in check. And as the new lives *and* new deaths grew in number, Shaikulud grew angrier and angrier. Her mind roiled with thoughts of what she would do to the User-that-is-not-a-user, sinister and malicious thoughts. And with each new thought, her eye grew brighter and brighter with hatred.

"You will soon be mine, Gameknight999!" she shouted to no one . . . to everyone.

CHAPTER 15
WELCOME TO THE JUNGLE

The NPCs moved quickly through the rest of the ice spikes biome, finding themselves in a grassy plains biome. Gameknight wished that the landscape were hillier to give them some protection from prying eyes, but as his friend Shawny was fond of saying, "It is what it is."

With the company running most of the time, they shot across the grassy plains with great haste. Pausing only occasionally to rest, they ran through most of the day. At night, the cavalry created two rings around those on foot; the wolves roaming outside of both. Occasionally they heard the moans of zombies, but they were usually far off. Any monster sounds, though, quickly drew a violent response from the wolves, keeping the creatures of the night far from the group.

As the sun rose on the second day, Gameknight could see something bright green on the horizon ahead of them. Off to the left and right, he could see steep mountains . . . likely an extreme hills biome.

"That looks like jungle ahead," Stitcher said.

She was walking next to him, his sister next to the young NPC. They had become fast friends during this adventure.

"I think you're right," Monet113 added.

"Watcher!" Gameknight yelled over his shoulder. "What do you see?"

An NPC with huge green eyes sprinted up to Gameknight's side. He stopped for a moment and peered at the band of green that lay before them, then raced to catch up with him again.

"Sure enough . . . it's jungle," Watcher said.

Stitcher and Monet both smiled.

"I can see the vines hanging down from the tree branches and the thick bushes around the base of the junglewood trees," Watcher continued. "There are numerous cocoa pods on the trees . . . we'll want to harvest those when we reach them."

"As long as we don't need to slow down," Gameknight said. "I feel that things will get a little crazy when we go in there."

Looking to the back of the army, Watcher suddenly stopped and stared at the western horizon. He then gasped, causing Gameknight to stop and move to his side.

"What is it?" the User-that-is-not-a-user asked.

"Something is coming toward us across these plains," Watcher said, his green eyes straining. "I can't quite make out what they are, but I'm sure that there are a lot of them, and they're coming fast. I can see a huge cloud of dust rising around them." He turned and faced Gameknight999.

"Should we stop and fight them?" asked Crafter, who was suddenly at his side, listening.

"No, we keep going," Gameknight said. "We learned something when we were battling back in the Nether that we must not forget. 'Speed is the essence of war.' It is important that we do not relearn that painful lesson."

Crafter nodded in agreement, then spun and continued to run toward the bright green horizon, Gameknight999 following close behind.

They crossed the rest of the rolling hills without incident and finally reached the edge of the jungle when the sun was at its zenith. Sheer mountains sat on either side of the jungle, the line of steep hills stretching out to the north and south. Anyone heading this way had no choice but to pass through the jungle if they wanted to continue their journey.

"Welcome to the jungle," Hunter said. "I'm sure it won't be fun 'n' games in there, so everyone stay sharp."

"Hunter's right," Gameknight added. "We don't have time to rest, so everyone stay close."

Gripping his enchanted sword tightly, Gameknight plunged into the undergrowth. Instantly, a wall of leaves and vines blocked his path. Pulling out his iron axe, he started to cut a path through the leafy terrain. Over his shoulder, he could see the other villagers had done the same; now a hundred axes were tearing into the jungle where necessary.

But even with all those blades cutting into trees and bushes, progress was slow. Some of the villagers tried to go around obstacles and quickly found themselves separated from the rest of the party.

"Where are you? I'm lost," yelled some villager.

"Over this way," yelled another.

Quickly, the NPCs became dispersed, separated by the thick junglewood trunks and lack of visibility.

"Crafter, we have to keep them all together somehow," Gameknight said. "You have any ideas?"

"I have a few," he said, smiling.

Moving to an open area, Crafter planted a small red and white striped rocket on the ground, then stepped back. It shot up into the air, leaving behind a trail of sparks, then exploded high over the treetops, displaying a shower of sparkling color.

"Excellent," Gameknight said.

Crafter beamed a huge smile.

"Everyone keep going!" Gameknight shouted. "Stay near Crafter's fireworks."

"Don't you think those fireworks will tell every monster where we are?" Hunter asked.

"They already know that we're here, I'm sure of it," Gameknight answered. "They're probably watching us right now."

Hunter spun around, drawing her sword.

"Relax," Gameknight said. "If they wanted to attack, they would. For some reason, they're waiting."

"Well, I'll be ready for them anyway," she replied as she turned and continued through the jungle.

Suddenly, an explosion sounded through the jungle, punctuated by a scream and the smell of sulfur.

"Creeper!" someone shouted.

Just then another one exploded a little closer.

"We can't even see them," Brewer shouted as she came running toward Gameknight. "I saw it just at the last instant and was able to get to cover, but their green and black color merged right in with all the vines and leaves."

"This is trouble," Digger said, his voice low so that only Gameknight999 could hear.

"I know what to do," Herder said as he came running to the front of the group. "We need more . . . many more friends."

"What are you talking about, Herder?" Gameknight asked.

But the youth didn't answer as he ran off into the jungle.

"We can't just stand here," Hunter said. "We'll be sitting ducks!"

"You're right," Gameknight answered, then yelled out commands for all to hear. "Everyone, run toward the east. Stay together and keep close to Crafter's fireworks!"

Turning, Gameknight started to run, going around obstacles when he could, using his axe when he had no other choice. Slowly, the collection of NPCs picked up speed, but their trek was still interrupted periodically by detonating creepers.

"We need to see where those creepers are coming from!" Gameknight exclaimed. "Hunter, you think you can get some of your archers up there on the treetops?"

"Piece of cake."

She gathered a couple of NPCs, then moved to the closest tree and started placing blocks of dirt around the dark trunk. Gameknight watched as she built a spiral staircase around the tree, carving through branches and leaves with her axe until she disappeared into the leafy canopy.

"You see anything?" Gameknight yelled.

"Oh yeah . . . I see plenty," she replied.

"Are you going to tell me, or just keep it to yourself?"

"I'm not sure you want to know what I'm seeing," she yelled from the treetops. "You want to good news or the bad news?"

"HUNTER!"

"OK, here's the bad news," she said, then came down a step or two so that Gameknight could see her. "There are about fifty to sixty creepers heading straight for us. That must have been what was following us across the grassy plains biome."

"What's the good news?" Gameknight asked.

"It's not a hundred creepers," she said as she laughed.

Gameknight growled in frustration.

"Hunter, get all the NPCs down here," Gameknight said, then turned to face Crafter. "Send up a bunch of fireworks, we need to get everyone together."

Crafter nodded, then placed rocket after rocket on the ground, their sparkling images bursting overhead.

"EVERYONE COME TO MY VOICE!" Gameknight shouted.

He then heard his sister's voice shouting as well as Stitcher's.

"EVERYONE OVER HERE," they shouted, bringing all the NPCs to Gameknight.

With their help, all the NPCs collected in a small clearing.

"Here's the situation," Gameknight explained. "A huge group of creepers is heading right for us. We can't fight them in this jungle; our cavalry has no mobility with all these trees and bushes. Our only chance is to clear an area and fight."

"Against sixty creepers? That's impossible," someone said.

"It doesn't matter," Gameknight replied. "We won't just give up. You can only accomplish what you can imagine, and I imagine that we can get through this . . . somehow. Now, let's get to work."

They all pulled out their axes and started cutting down bushes and leafy trees. Soon they had a large clearing in front of them. Using some of the trees and bushes as defensive structures, then carving spaces behind them for defenders to stand, they hoped the obstacles would give them some protection against the creeper's explosive touch. Archers climbed high up in the trees, hoping to shoot at the creepers before they came close, but it was hard to get a clear shot.

They were desperate and Gameknight knew it.

Look what I have done, Gameknight thought. *I led my friends . . . no, my family, into this perilous situation, and now many of them are going to die. I hate this responsibility, it's too . . .*

Just then, another thought echoed in his head, but the strange thing was that it wasn't his voice. It was that strange mystical voice he'd heard at the stronghold.

Be strong, User-that-is-not-a-user, and have faith in your friends. Being responsible doesn't mean doing everything yourself; it means asking for help when you need help. Have faith and be patient.

The voice then faded away, leaving him with his own thoughts.

What was that? What did it mean . . . have faith and be patient? I can't just . . .

Suddenly, the scurrying of short stubby feet pulled him from his thought and brought him back to *the now.* He could see a massive collection of creepers enter the clearing. Hunter may have been wrong . . . it could have been a hundred. However many there were, they were too numerous to count, and they could surely destroy them all.

"Everyone RUN!" someone yelled.

"NO!" Gameknight shouted even louder.

He wasn't sure what to say, but then something unexpected came from his mouth.

"HAVE FAITH . . . AND BE PATIENT!"

But the creepers were not patient. They moved into the clearing, their tiny feet kicking up a thin layer of dust from the ground. Archers started firing their arrows, but they did little against this many creepers. And as they closed in, the lead creeper stared straight at Gameknight999 with cold black eyes overflowing with hatred, and then the creature started to glow as a hissing filled the air. Then all the other creepers stared to hiss as well.

All Gameknght999 could think was, *Is this the end?*

CHAPTER 16

WOLFMAN

Suddenly, out of the dense jungle sprinted Herder with a huge collection of cats following close behind. There must have been at least fifty of the spotted felines; some of them tamed cats while some were still wild ocelots. The clowder of cats bolted into the clearing, charging directly at the creepers, their meows and yowls drowning out the hissing monsters.

As soon as the creepers saw the cats, they stopped their ignition process and ran back into the dense jungle, the cats close on their heels.

"WOLFMAN!" the NPCs cheered.

Herder beamed as he waved at the villagers, then turned to follow the cats.

"HERDER, COME BACK!" Gameknight999 yelled.

The lanky youth stopped running and turned, staring back at the User-that-is-not-a-user, a confused look on his face. He then ran toward his friend and stopped by his side.

"Where are you going?" Gameknight asked.

"I was gonna check on my friends," he said.

"There's a huge army of creepers out there," Hunter said as she moved to his side. "You think going out there alone is the best idea?"

Herder looked at Hunter, confusion on his face.

"But I wouldn't be alone," he said. "I'd have my cats with me."

Hunter shook her head and laughed, then patted him on the back. Turning, she faced the other NPCs and held his hand high up into the air.

"WOLFMAN!" she yelled.

"WOLFMAN!" the villagers responded with glee.

"We have to get out of here," Gameknight said, then yelled to the other villagers. "Everyone keep heading toward the east!"

"And stay together!" Crafter shouted.

"Let's go!" Gameknight shouted. They continued on their journey.

Scanning the jungle, he saw Monet easily in her multi-colored armor, her bright fluorescent blue hair spilling down her back. Next to her, he saw Stitcher, her red hair standing out in contrast to Monet's electric blue.

With a circle of wolves around them, and another circle of cats around that, the group was able to move through the jungle without further creeper incursions. They stumbled upon a collection of spiders here and there, but with archers running along the treetops and warriors on the ground, they were not in too much trouble. Some of the villagers took injuries from the spiders, but all survived the encounters.

As the sun slowly settled down near the horizon, Gameknight thought he could see blue through the spaces between trees. The trickling of running water could be heard over the sounds of the jungle, waves crashing on a beach adding to the symphony.

And then suddenly, they were through the dense jungle, and out in the open. Before them stood a cool river that curved this way and that as it snaked its way across the landscape, draining into a massive ocean. Just on the other side of the river was an ancient looking structure made of cobblestone and mossy cobblestone, vines hanging down the sides as if it hadn't been used in centuries.

"We made it," Crafter said, relief in his voice.

He placed a hand on Gameknight's shoulder, then patted him on the back.

"You did it . . . you got us here," Crafter said.

"I didn't do anything," Gameknight replied. "I just kept going . . . that's all."

"Sometimes surrender is easier than persistence," Crafter said. "But your reluctance to quit kept everyone going."

"I don't know . . . I'm just glad we're here," Gameknight said. "But we aren't done yet . . . look."

He pointed to the sun that was just starting to move behind the junglewood trees behind them. Its yellow face could be seen between the branches of the trees, but it was getting perilously near the horizon.

"It will be dark soon," Gameknight said in a low voice. "The real battle will start tonight. We must be prepared."

"Everyone will do what they must," Crafter reassured, "no matter how tired they are."

Gameknight nodded his head, then turned and looked for Digger. He found the big NPC near the edge of the river, washing his hands. Gameknight moved to his side.

"Digger, I need you to prepare the defenses," Gameknight said. "I'm going into the temple to see if we can find this Oracle. I know Herobrine will throw everything he has against us . . . we must be prepared with some surprises of our own."

Reaching into his inventory, Digger pulled out a stack of redstone dust with his right hand, then drew a stack of pistons with his left. Looking up at Gameknight999, the big NPC smiled.

"Where did you get that?" Gameknight asked.

Digger pointed to a chest that was nestled under a bush, a redstone torch next to it, making it stand out against the green foliage.

"I just found it there," Digger explained. "It was as if it were just waiting for us."

Gameknight smiled, then looked up into the air and mouthed, *THANK YOU, SHAWNY.*

"OK, we have a lot to do," Gameknight said as he waded through the river. Turning, he faced the NPCs. "We have defenses to set up, traps to build, and a war to prepare for . . . all before sunset, so let's get to it!"

"Yeah!" cheered the NPCs as they charged through the river and stood on the opposite bank, the ancient jungle temple standing before them . . . waiting.

CHAPTER 17

THE ORACLE

They stepped into the musty temple cautiously, with eyes sharp and senses focused. Gameknight knew that jungle temples were always rigged with traps; there would be tripwires attached to dispensers, and pressure plates set to trigger pistons, and more . . . There was no telling how many traps would be in this ancient structure; they had to be careful.

Crafter moved into the temple first, planting torches on the ground as we went. His sharp eyes searched every part of the cobblestone passageway, looking for anything out of place. Following close behind were Gameknight, Stitcher, Monet, Hunter, and Herder, each also planting torches to drive away the shadows . . . and their fear.

The entrance led to a floor with two stairways going up and one wide staircase going down to the floor below.

"Hunter, Stitcher, check the floor above," Gameknight said.

"Couldn't there be traps up there?" Monet asked. Clearly she was concerned for her friend.

"No, the traps are always down below," Gameknight answered. "You go with them."

Excitedly, she ran after them, taking the steps two at a time.

"It's all empty up here," Hunter shouted from the top floor. "But it would be a good place to put some archers."

"Do it," Gameknight said. "Also, have someone put some more holes in the walls so that we can get a larger field of fire. Stitcher, get someone to help."

The young girl ran down the steps, her red hair streaming behind her like luminous flames.

"Wait," Gameknight said, stopping Stitcher in her tracks. "We also need to get some archers on the roof. Get one of the Masons to put some steps in and have fortifications built up there . . . you got it?"

She nodded her head then took off.

"Hunter, come on down," Gameknight said.

The older sister came bounding down the steps with Monet right behind.

"Let's go down," Crafter said. "Everyone stay close and don't touch anything."

The group went carefully down the steps until the stairway ended in a narrow corridor that went off to the right. Turning the corner, the group followed the passage until it ended, and then turned to the right again. Crafter stopped at the corner and looked down the next long hallway. At the other end, he could see a chest that sat against a vine-covered wall.

"A chest!" Monet exclaimed. "There could be something magical, maybe some enchanted armor."

She started to run down the hallway, but Gameknight caught her arm and held fast, jerking her to a stop.

"What?" she whined.

"It's a trap," Gameknight said.

"I don't see anything," she complained.

"Exactly," Crafter added.

Moving carefully forward, Crafter led them down the left side of the hallway, so that they weren't directly in front of the vine-covered blocks. Creeping forward ever so slowly, the young NPC peered into the small nooks created by the alternating blocks that lined the bottom of the walls.

"Here it is," Crafter said as he pulled out his pickaxe.

Chopping at something that was hidden in the shadows, Crafter pulled out a tripwire mechanism. Moving further down the passage, they could now see the redstone that was wired to the vine-covered block.

"Monet, you see the black hole in that block?" Crafter asked.

She nodded.

He cut away the rest of the vines, and Monet gasped. They could all see a dispenser at the end of the red stone circuit. Inside, they found it filled with stacks and stacks of arrows.

"Perfect," Hunter said as she reached in and took all the arrows. "The archers could use these . . . some of them are getting low."

Stuffing them into her inventory, Hunter then knelt next to the chest that sat below the dispenser and slowly opened it. The hinges creaked and groaned from the years of neglect. Pushing hard to get it open, Hunter gasped at what she saw within.

Inside the chest, they found a single diamond and three iron ingots. There was also an iron pickaxe that sparkled with magical enchantments.

Gameknight reached in for the pick. The waves of iridescent magic flowed up and down the tool, illuminating the corridor with sapphire light. Gameknight wished there had been more diamonds so that he could repair his armor; it was still badly damaged from his last encounter with Herobrine, but it didn't do any good to wish for what wasn't there.

Placing the pickaxe into his inventory, Gameknight closed the lid, then turned as he heard footsteps echoing down the next corridor. It was his sister, Monet. She'd walked through the adjacent passage that led off to the right.

"Look, switches," she said.

Gameknight could see three switches on the wall at the far end of the cobblestone-lined hallway. Vines had grown down the wall above the switches, but had been trimmed neatly to allow the switches to still work.

"What do the switches do?" Monet asked.

"Those usually do nothing," Gameknight explained. "They just move some pistons so that it sounds like they are opening doors or setting traps, but they don't do anything."

"Let's see," Monet said as she flipped one of the levers.

"Nooo!" Crafter yelled, but it was too late.

Monet placed her hand on the first lever and flipped it down. A click sounded as a piston moved somewhere beneath them, triggering additional pistons. The rumbling sound of stone grinding against stone resonated throughout the temple as the passageway became dark. The light streaming in down the main staircase slowly dimmed until the stairs were completely encased in shadows.

Running to the stairway, Gameknight found the descending entrance completely blocked; a new wall of bedrock was now closing off their exit. It was impossible to tunnel through bedrock, even with diamond pickaxes . . . which meant they could not escape. Returning to his friends, Gameknight999 scowled at his sister.

"Great, we're trapped in here," he said to the others, then turned to his sister. "Thanks!"

Monet looked away from her brother and at the ground.

Why does she have to be so impulsive? he thought. *Why can't she be like me and carefully make plans and calculate what might happen before acting?*

He shook his head as he glared at her. Following her gaze, he could see that Monet was looking at the floor. Clearly she felt bad . . . but then he noticed something else. There was a small stone button near the floor beneath the three switches. Stone buttons were difficult to see when placed on cobblestone, and this one was placed right near the floor as well, making it even harder to see. Moving to his sister's side, he pointed down at the button.

"Look at this, Crafter," Gameknight said.

Crafter moved next to Monet, then knelt on the ground. With a puff of air, he blew away the dust that covered these lower blocks, revealing the stone switch.

"You ever see one of these in a jungle temple?" Gameknight asked.

Crafter shook his head.

"There is . . . ahh . . . something else here," Herder said as he moved to Monet's other side.

Reaching up, Herder pulled at the vines that covered the walls above the switches. When the tangle of plants fell to the ground, they revealed four signs, one above each switch, and one higher up on the wall. There was writing on each sign.

"What do they say?" Gameknight asked.

"We need more light," Herder replied.

Crafter planted a torch next to the signs.

"One says *BLUE*, the next says *RED,* and the last says *YELLOW*," Herder read.

Each of those signs was placed directly above a switch.

"What about the one above those?" Crafter asked.

"It doesn't make any sense," Herder said as he squinted to see the letters. "It says, *WHAT ARE THE COLORS OF SUPERMAN'S CAPE?*" The lanky NPC turned to Crafter, a confused look on his face. "What does it mean?"

"I don't know?" Crafter answered.

"It's a riddle that only a user could answer," the Gameknight replied with a smile. "We're trapped in here until we can answer the riddle . . . and it's easy."

Stepping up to the switches, he gently pushed the others out of the way and flipped the red switch up, moving the other levers to the down position. Kneeling, Gameknight reached for the stone button.

"Superman's cape is red," the User-that-is-not-a-user said triumphantly with a self-satisfied grin, then pushed the stone button.

"Nooo!" shouted Monet, but it was too late.

The sound of stone grinding against stone filled the passage as the floor just behind them slowly slid away, revealing a pool of lava underneath. The heat from the molten stone blasted the companions in the face, causing small cubes of sweat to form and trickle down their flat cheeks. Moving as far from the lava as they could, the NPCs and Monet looked up at Gameknight999.

"It's easy, huh?" Hunter asked.

"That was the wrong answer," Monet said with an exasperated tone.

"What are you talking about?" Gameknight asked. "It's red."

"Nope," Monet replied.

"But I've seen all the movies," Gameknight said, "and read a bunch of the comics . . . Superman's cape is RED!"

"Nope," she said again, this time with a knowing smile on her face.

"Oh yeah?" Gameknight snapped. "Then if you're so smart, what color is it?"

Monet reached down and reset the switches, then flipped up the red switch.

Gameknight smiled.

Then she flipped up the yellow switch.

Gameknight looked confused and stared at his sister.

"The "S" on his cape is yellow!" she said proudly, then reached down and pressed the button.

"Before you press that, you should realize that we don't have any place to run to," Crafter said. "If you're wrong, then likely the floor under us will fall away and we'll end up trying to swim in lava."

Monet looked up at her friends, the confident look on her face starting to fade, but then she pushed the button. The sound of stone grinding against stone filled the corridor again, but the floor didn't move. Instead, the wall next to them slid sideways, revealing a torch-lit stairway that plunged deep under the temple.

"YES!" Monet exclaimed.

"Apparently you were right," Gameknight said reluctantly.

"What?" Monet asked, wanting to hear it again.

"You heard me!" he snapped, then headed down the lit stairway, Crafter following close behind.

Monet stood there and smiled at Hunter and Herder for an instant, then followed the young NPC with Herder on her heels, Hunter bringing up the rear.

They moved down the steps, probably plunging down at least fifty blocks before reaching some kind of brightly lit room.

Moving cautiously to the entrance, Gameknight peered into the underground chamber. What he found was ornately designed, like a throne room for a king. Tall pillars of mossy cobblestone stretched up from the floor to greet the stone ceiling that was probably fifteen blocks high overhead. Around the edges of the room were torches set in every third block, with glowstone cubes placed throughout the chamber, adding to the illumination. Off to the left side of the chamber, Gameknight could see another passageway that led off to some other room. Sounds came from that passage . . . sounds that he couldn't quite recognize and that made him a little afraid.

Across the center of the massive room were complex structures built of every color imaginable. Emerald blocks lined what looked like a walkway that stretched the distance from the stairway to the tall platform at the other end of the room. Blocks of lapis filled in the walkway, with gold and iron cubes mixed in to add contrast to the complex pattern of colors.

Gameknight could hear Monet gasp when she finally reached the entrance. Turning to look at his sister, Gameknight saw a look of awe on her square face, her eyes filled with wonder at all the colors. For her, this was the finest of feasts.

But then a tapping sound echoed through the chamber. Gameknight could tell that it came from the raised platform on the far side, from behind the structure on the platform that could only be described as a throne. The tapping grew louder as an old woman, older than any NPC he'd ever seen, stepped out from behind the throne.

"I have been expecting you, Gameknight999," the old woman said in a scratchy voice. "You brought your friends, I see . . . I should have expected this."

She moved across the raised platform, and slowly, carefully, down the stone steps that led to the ground. The cane that she used looked to be carved from some kind of ancient wood, the end of the stick capped with iron. She used it to help her walk, the metal end tapping on the ground with each step. Her long gray hair swayed back and forth as she strained to walk down the steps. Moving along the emerald-lined path, she slowly traversed half the length of the room and stood there . . . waiting.

"Well?" she asked. "Are you going to just stand there, or are you going to come in?"

Gameknight looked at Crafter, then Hunter. They both shrugged, uncertain what to do. Turning to look back at the old woman, the User-that-is-not-a-user cautiously moved into the chamber and crossed the colorful floor until he was standing before her, three blocks away. Without having to look back, he could tell that his friends had followed.

"It is nice to finally meet you, Gameknight999." The old woman turned toward Monet. "Ahh . . . I see you have your sister with you. Welcome, Monet113." She then turned to Crafter and Hunter. "Crafter, we finally meet in person. I have heard so much about you over the years. And lastly, Hunter, the great warrior . . . I have watched you many times in the Land of Dreams; you are a most diligent protector . . . I commend you, but I had hoped to also meet your younger sister. Oh well, perhaps later."

The companions stared at the old woman, not knowing what to say.

How did this woman know all our names? Gameknight thought.

"I know your names, Gameknight999, because the Creator, Notch, constructed me to be part of Minecraft," she explained. "I'm not just another segment of code running around out there. I am part of the fabric that holds all this together. I create the music of Minecraft that you all hear when your mind is still. Notch created me to be part of the entire system, so that I could protect the servers and the digital lives that live within them. And there is a threat to these lives, you know his name as Herobrine. He infected these servers a hundred years ago, and now it is time he was controlled. Herobrine is a virus that can no longer be allowed to run around, unchecked. I am the anti-virus."

She then took a step closer to Gameknight999 and peered into his worried eyes.

"User-that-is-not-a-user and his trusted companions, welcome to my lair," she said with a rough, aged voice, holding her arms out wide. "I am the Oracle, and the *real* battle for Minecraft is about to start."

CHAPTER 18

THE WEAPON

We have a lot of questions," Gameknight said.

"I'm sure you do," the Oracle responded.

Gameknight looked at Crafter, his friends' eyes wide and mouth hanging slightly open. He looked stunned to be standing before this piece of Minecraft history.

"Crafter . . . you have any questions?" Gameknight said a little louder.

"OK, here's the deal," Hunter said as she stepped in front of Crafter and came closer to the old woman.

But before she could finish, a growling sound came from the dark tunnel to their left. They were angry sounds, not just from one creature, but many of them. Instinctively, Gameknight reached for his sword and Hunter drew her bow.

"You do not need your weapons," the Oracle said. "You are quite safe in my temple."

"How do you know that?" Hunter asked. "What about those growls?" She pointed to the shadowy tunnel.

"This is my domain . . . not his," the Oracle stated as if she were reciting some universal truth. "You are all completely safe while you are in here with me."

Hunter looked at Gameknight, then slowly put away her bow.

"So . . . we're here because of . . ." Hunter said but was interrupted.

"I know why you have come," the Oracle said.

"Oh really?" Hunter asked.

"Yes," the old woman replied. "You have come here because of your nemesis, Herobrine."

"You know where he is?" Crafter asked, finally come back to his senses.

"Yes," she replied. "I can sense him through the tree leaves. Many, many years ago, I modified the code for the trees so I could track his position, using the leaves to sense his presence. In addition, when I created my wolves, I sent them out to watch for Herobrine across all the server planes, attacking him at every opportunity."

Herder instantly perked up at the mention of the wolves.

"Yes, Herder," the Oracle said, "I created your little friends."

Herder's eyes grew wide in amazement, then flicked toward the dark tunnel that pierced the wall of the chamber.

"Of course," she answered him, somehow hearing his unasked question. "Go visit with my friends. They will accept you as all animals do in Minecraft."

The lanky youth took a step toward the tunnel, then turned back and looked at Gameknight999.

"Go on," Gameknight said. "We're OK here, for now."

Giving him a huge grin, Herder sprinted off across the chamber and into the dark tunnel. Instantly, Gameknight could hear the barking of what sounded like a huge pack of wolves, their excited howls resonating throughout the chamber.

Looking back to the Oracle, Gameknight saw that she was smiling.

"He is a good boy," the old woman said. "You have done well, accepting him as he is."

"He is part of our community," Crafter said proudly, "and a trusted friend."

The Oracle smiled and nodded her head.

"This is all well and good, but we didn't come here to play with a bunch of dogs," Herder said. "We need something to help us defeat Herobrine. I'm sure his whole army is on their way toward us right now."

"They are already here," the Oracle said. "They were here before your journey even began."

"What?" Hunter snapped as she fitted an arrow to her bow.

"Relax, you are safe within these walls," the Oracle said.

"But what about our friends outside these walls?" Gameknight asked. "We have to protect them, and we must defeat Herobrine. He wants to escape from the Minecraft servers and move into the physical world . . . I cannot allow that."

"I know," the Oracle responded.

"And I don't know how to defeat him," the User-that-is-not-a-user explained. "He's too fast with those teleportation powers. I never know where he is or where he will attack next."

"I know," she said again.

"We need something that will help us destroy him," Gameknight said, now pleading. "The safety of the physical world and the safety of Minecraft are paramount, but we don't know how to stop him."

"I know."

"You keep saying 'I know . . . I know,' but I don't hear you saying that you'll help us," Hunter said. "Was this just a waste of time coming here? There are monsters on their way here, you said so yourself, and they need to be destroyed. But first we need a way to take care of Herobrine. Are you going to help?"

"Long have I watched you, Hunter," the Oracle said, then sighed. "A terrible thing . . . what happened to your family. You are now filled with such hate and violence that eventually your thirst for vengeance will consume the wonderful person you are until all that is left is pain and death. You walk a dangerous path."

"What?" Hunter asked, confused. "This isn't about me, this is about killing all those monsters."

"You seek violence before you seek understanding," the Oracle said. "These creatures are not coming here by choice; they are being driven here by Herobrine."

"I don't care why they are coming . . . they are monsters, so they should be destroyed. We cannot trust them or live with them or leave them alone because eventually they will attack us," Hunter yelled, taking a step closer to the old NPC.

"Perhaps they think the same thing about you," the Oracle replied.

"Who cares what they think? They are monsters and we have nothing in common with them!"

"You only have nothing in common when you don't look," the old woman replied, her scratchy voice sounding aged and wise. "Hunter, you have mastered the Land of Dreams as no other has in the history of Minecraft. For that I am proud of you."

The old woman then glanced at Monet113 and smiled a knowing smile. Monet looked away quickly as if caught doing something wrong. Gameknight looked down at his sister, then back to the Oracle, confused.

"But I do not have a secret weapon that will defeat Herobrine for you," the old woman said.

"Well, this was a great idea coming here!" Hunter snapped, glaring at Crafter and Gameknight999.

"However," the Oracle continued, "I have half the weapon you need."

Reaching into her inventory, she pulled out what looked like an egg. It was shaped like one of the spider's eggs that Gameknight had seen in Shaikulud's nest, round at one end, narrowing slightly at the other. But this one was shaded a rosy color, almost a light pink, but with spots all across the surface. Holding it carefully with both hands, the Oracle extended it toward the User-that-is-not-a-user.

"What is it?" Gameknight asked.

"Hope," she replied.

Stepping forward, he reached out and took it from the old wrinkled hands. Inspecting its surface, Gameknight999 expected to see some kind of button or switch he could push to make it transform into something else . . . something useful . . . but saw none. Turning it over in his hands, he looked carefully at the surface, then held it out for Crafter to take.

"NO!" snapped the Oracle. "This weapon is for the hands of the User-that-is-not-a-user. Only he can wield it, if he can figure out how."

Gameknight looked at Crafter, hoping his wise friend would give him some kind of answer, but his big blue eyes showed the confusion that Gameknight felt. Looking to Hunter, Gameknight thought he might ask her if she had any ideas.

"They cannot tell you anything," the Oracle said, somehow hearing his very thoughts. Then she raised her voice so that it resonated throughout the chamber. "Gameknight999, this is a weapon that can only be used once. If it is used at the wrong time, then it will fail and you will fail. If it is used incorrectly, then it will fail and you will fail."

She gazed into Gameknight's eyes with an intensity that made him want to look away, but for some reason he could not. With their eyes locked, she leaned forward slightly, then continued in a low, ominous voice.

"You must have the wisdom to know *when* and *how* to use this weapon. The entire world, both Minecraft and physical, teeters on a razor's edge, and any mistakes will plunge both into misery and despair. Everything depends on the wisdom of the User-that-is-not-a-user."

And then, as her words echoed within Gameknight's mind, the Oracle grew silent.

"Well . . . no pressure here," Hunter said with a smile.

"Hunter, be quiet!" Crafter snapped.

Gameknight looked down at the weapon in his hands and imagined how he might use it. Closing his eyes, he let his senses drift across the egg, feeling for its secrets . . . but he came up with nothing. No ideas on how to use it, no clever tricks, no wisdom . . . nothing.

Shaking his head, he carefully put the egg into his inventory.

"OK, you know what to do?" Hunter asked.

Uncertain, Gameknight lowered his gaze to the ground, embarrassed at his lack of understanding . . . his failure.

"Perhaps he will come to understand, over time," the Oracle said.

"You're a big help," Hunter snapped, her voice dripping with sarcasm.

"Hunter . . . be respectful," Crafter snapped.

"Well?" she replied as she spun around and headed back to the stairs, her red hair flinging through the air like a crimson wave.

Stopping at the foot of the stairs, Hunter glanced over her shoulder at the Oracle.

"We need to get back to our friends on the surface," she said as she shifted her bow from her right hand to her left. "Is the passageway open?"

The Oracle closed her eyes for a moment. The sound of stone grinding against stone reverberated through the temple for a moment, then stopped.

"You can now leave," the old woman said.

"Great," Hunter replied, then turned to face her companions. "Let's get to the surface. We need to make sure everything is ready when Herobrine gets here." She then pointed at Gameknight999 with her bow. "You need to figure out how to make that weapon work by then or it's game over . . . you got that?"

Gameknight nodded, fear and uncertainty filling his entire being.

How am I going to do this? he thought. *I don't have the faintest idea what to do with this egg-thing. All of them are relying on me, expecting me to be some kind of expert. But I'm not . . . I'm just a kid. What am I going to do?*

Be patient and have faith, a voice said from somewhere else in his mind.

Turning, he looked at the Oracle and found that she had a wry smile on her face.

"What do you mean 'Have faith'?!" he snapped, frustrated at her lack of help.

"Have faith in those around you," the Oracle said. "Even the smallest and youngest have something to contribute. Aid will come to you from the most unexpected of places."

"You talk in riddles," Gameknight complained as he turned and followed Hunter up the stairs, Monet and Crafter fast on his heels.

As he climbed the stairs, Gameknight looked one last time upon the Oracle. Her long gray hair seemed to be glowing in the torchlight of the ornate cavern. But as he gazed at her, he could feel his own doubt circling him like a pack of wolves ready to attack.

CHAPTER 19

THE JAWS SNAP SHUT

When Gameknight999 walked out of the temple, he found the landscape clothed in darkness; the sun was now completely hidden behind the horizon. That concerned him, but what worried him more were the looks on all the NPCs' faces; they were filled with panic and desperation . . . as if the battle was already lost.

"What's wrong?" he asked as he stepped out of the musty entrance.

"The scouts say that there are two huge armies of spiders heading straight for us," Teacher said.

Looking back at the temple, Gameknight could see Digger and Crafter emerging from the entrance. In the darkness, the torches that had been placed around the structure made it stand out like some kind of sacred monument, the torches driving away the shadow of night.

Surrounding the temple, Gameknight could see the villagers had built a series of walls. Stone, brick, cobblestone, and dirt were used all around their position; anything that would make a useful obstacle for the monsters that were slowly closing in on them. Off to the sides of the temple, he could see tall archer towers that had been built out of cobblestone and dirt, a cluster of sharp arrows pointing outward from its peak. Near the base of each tower were TNT cannons, each pointing in a different direction so as to cover a larger field of fire. Around the cannons, the villagers had put large areas of soul sand; the rusty blocks would hopefully slow the advance of any attackers.

I wonder where they got all that soul sand? Gameknight thought. He figured the answer was probably his friend, Shawny.

Gameknight smiled.

In front of the temple, the NPCs had cleared a huge part of the jungle away, making it necessary for the monsters to cross a large open area. Torches had been planted all throughout the clearing, giving the villagers brightly lit targets at which to shoot. The flaming lights flickered in the wind, painting the landscape with a curious brush; large circles of golden illumination dotted the shadowy landscape like huge bright splotches on a painter's canvas. Hopefully, those circles of light would make the monsters easier to see . . . and destroy.

Woven throughout the clearing were wide bands of gravel. Gameknight knew that the villagers had likely made redstone traps as they had in their own village. He could see a building made of cobblestone right near the temple entrance. Inside, he could see levers mounted on the walls, thin lines of redstone leading to each. Across the windows of the structure were iron bars. They would allow the operator to watch the battle but be free from attack.

The villagers had been busy.

"You all did fantastic!" Gameknight yelled.

The NPCs beamed as they wiped their sweaty brows. Many were still adding blocks to walls while another group was carving a deep channel into the river that surrounded the temple, making it more difficult to wade through.

Suddenly, Hunter was at his side.

"They did a good job, didn't they?" she asked.

"Yes they did," Gameknight answered, but then he leaned close and lowered his voice. "The problem is that we're stuck here. We have no mobility, no ability to change the location of the battle. Essentially we are trapped with our backs against the sea." He looked around to make sure that nobody else could hear him. "Herobrine can keep sending wave after wave of monsters at us, and we can't do anything but fight until we are slowly whittled down to nothing. I've seen how many monsters he has for this fight, and we can't win."

Hunter looked at him and then gave him one of her crazed smiles.

"Hey . . . have faith," she said. "Look at all these people around you. Can't you see the hunger in their eyes?" Hunter then raised her voice so that all could hear. "Herobrine can send as many creatures as he wants against these defenses. They will crash against our walls and be pushed back over and over."

Many of the NPCs cheered.

"You see?" she said as she turned back to Gameknight999. "No big deal."

"What are you talking about?" he said quietly. "It's not the spiders that concern me, even though I've seen how many they have, and surviving that army will be a miracle. But let's say, just for fun, that we are able to defeat the spiders. What do we do about Herobrine?"

He then leaned close and whispered in her ear. "With his teleportation powers, he could just zip around and attack us one at a time, and we'd have no way to stop him." Gameknight then peered into her dark brown eyes, her curly red hair lit by a nearby torch and creating a crimson halo around her square head. "What am I going to do?"

"You're going to do what you always do," she said.

"And what's that?"

"You'll figure it out at the last second, and then do something crazy that will save the day," Hunter explained. "That's what you do . . . that's what makes you the User-that-is-not-a-user. So you got nothing to worry about. Just be patient and wait for that inspiration that always seems to come when everything looks the bleakest. Though I wouldn't mind if you figured it out a little earlier."

She smiled and slapped him on the back, then ran off, laughing, her enchanted bow casting off a blue iridescent glow in the darkness.

Turning back to the temple, he found Monet standing near the entrance, Stitcher at her side. Running to them, he caught the pair just as they were about to run off and take up position amidst the defenders.

"Monet, Stitcher . . . wait!" Gameknight yelled as he approached.

"What's up, bro?" his sister asked.

"Where are you two going?" he asked.

"We have a nice spot staked out up in the archer tower on the left," Stitcher said as she pulled out her bow. Waves of magic rippled along its length, shading her face with a blue glow.

"Not Monet," Gameknight said.

Turning, he found that his sister had pulled her bow out as well, and it too was enchanted.

"How did you get that?" he asked. "I saw Hunter and she had her own bow."

"Some of the scouts came across a few skeletons," Monet113 explained. "One of them had this nice weapon, and they figured I could use it."

Gameknight nodded his head, but then grabbed her arm as she tried to walk off.

"No you don't," he commanded. "You aren't going out there. Dad made me responsible for you whether I like it or not, and out there in the middle of this battle will be the most dangerous place to be."

"You still don't trust me, do you?" Monet asked as she glared at her brother, refusing to back down.

"It's not about trust, it's about responsibility. Dad put me in charge because he had to be gone . . . as usual. I don't want this responsibility, but I'm stuck with it. Now, I'm going to give you a task, and if you don't listen to me, then I'll have one of the NPCs make sure you are put somewhere safe."

Looking to his right, he caught the eye of Smithy and motioned him to come near. The big NPC with the dusty apron ran to his side and waited patiently. Monet glanced at the blacksmith, then sighed and nodded her head.

"Excellent," Gameknight said. "Now, your job is to guard the Oracle. Go back into the temple and stay in there until I call for you."

"But I can help!" she shouted.

"No offense, Monet, but what difference could one arrow make in this battle? Look around you." He gestured to the NPCs finishing up their preparations. "These villagers are ready for what is about to happen; it has been a part of their lives for years. But you . . . you know nothing about war, about fighting. Your one arrow will make no difference in this battle. Now do as I asked."

"But . . ." she complained, but Gameknight turned and glanced at Smithy. The blacksmith took a step forward and glared down at Monet113.

"Fine!" she snapped and sulked back into the temple.

After watching his sister slowly shuffle into the temple, Gameknight turned and faced Stitcher.

"You know, you're wrong about her," Stitcher said.

"What do you mean?" Gameknight asked. "I have to take care of her, that's my responsibility. So what else can I do other than put her somewhere safe?"

I hate having all this responsibility! he thought.

"First of all, there is no place here that is safe," Stitcher said. "And second, taking care of her doesn't mean putting her in a box. Taking care of her means treating her with respect and letting her prove her own worth, not just to you, but to herself as well. What you've done is made her insignificant, and that's worse than putting her in some danger." She paused to pull an arrow out of her inventory and fit it to her bow. "You should have more faith in your sister, just like I had faith in you."

And then she spun around and ran off toward the archer tower. He wanted to go after her, but a scream from the jungle stopped him from moving.

"THEY'RE COMING! THEY'RE COMING! THEY'RE . . ." The voice was suddenly, violently cut off.

It was one of the Watchers. Digger had positioned them in the treetops, with mounted scouts placed throughout the jungle. The sound had caused all the NPCs to take up their arms as they fell into their defensive positions. Gameknight could see the archers in the towers fit arrows to their bows. NPCs placed torches along the defensive walls as they drew their weapons, making sure they could see well in the darkness. Those manning the cannons all picked up stacks of TNT and readied their artillery. Warriors mounted their horses, then drew their swords that shined in the light of a full moon.

All of the pieces on their side of the game board were ready, but for some reason, it all seemed wrong to Gameknight999. He was missing something here, but couldn't see it. Looking across their defenses, he looked for Crafter, wanting to ask him what he was missing, but it was too late.

"THE SPIDERS ARE HERE!" a horseman shouted as he rode out of the jungle, his armor cracked and scratched.

Gameknight could see more horsemen moving between the trees, trying to escape from the foliage, but it seemed as if some kind of dark tide swallowed them up; a clicking wave that had multiple red eyes and a thirst for violence. The riders' yells for help tore at the defenders, but they all knew that there was nothing that could be done.

Before them, a gigantic wave of spiders flowed out of the jungle, the shadowy bodies blending in with the darkness of night, their eyes glowing bright. The creatures emerged, but then stopped at the edge of the tree line. There were cave spiders by the hundreds intermingled with the gigantic black spiders. Some of the spiders were smaller, just hatchlings, but with razor sharp claws and venomous fangs. There were so many that Gameknight999 couldn't even count them. On the top of the sheer cliff that overlooked the temple, Gameknight could see one spider, larger than all the rest, slowly move up to the edge and peer down on them. This spider had bright purple eyes that burned with an unquenchable hatred for the NPCs. Gameknight knew that this was the spider that had been haunting his dreams; Shaikulud . . . Herobrine's creation.

Gameknight could see the spider queen look down on her forces, and it almost looked as if she were smiling. Following her gaze, he could see that they were completely surrounded. There were spiders not only directly in front of them, but also on their flanks, sealing them up against the ocean shore that was maybe twenty blocks behind the temple. Shaikulud had trapped them, and the jaws of the trap were about to snap shut.

The User-that-is-not-a-user didn't know what to do. There were so many spiders; so much hatred . . . on both sides. He hoped that a solution would appear within his mind, as Hunter had said, but the answer was completely missing . . . he had nothing.

So, for lack of a better idea, Gameknight999 drew his enchanted sword, moved to the front of their defenses and held his weapon up high. Drawing in the biggest breath his square lungs could hold, he yelled out with all his might, his cry joined by every NPC.

"FOR MINECRAFT!"

And then he gripped the hilt of his sword firmly, and waited.

CHAPTER 20

THE BATTLE FOR THE JUNGLE TEMPLE

From atop the sheer cliff that looked down upon the temple, Gameknight heard a screechy clicking sound that pierced through the noise of the defenders and the sounds of the approaching spiders. It brought an eerie silence to the soon-to-be battlefield and raised the NPC's tension to the point of breaking. All eyes shifted to the spider queen that looked down upon the villagers, her purple eyes blazing with hatred, her body lit with pale moonlight.

Gameknight could see her multiple eyes taking note of her enemy's defenses. She then turned and looked at the spiders that milled about near the edge of the clearing. Finally, she focused her hideous stare directly at the User-that-is-not-a-user. He could feel all those eyes boring down on him, amplifying his fear. He looked away. Suddenly, Hunter was at his side, her reassuring hand on his shoulder. And then Digger was on his other shoulder, his big pickaxe held over his shoulder. Their shoulders brushed against his own ever so slightly, and he could feel the strength and courage in the two NPCs.

I won't be afraid of that monster, he thought, even as uncertainty crept into his mind. *What if I can't defeat her, what if they are too many spiders, what if . . .* and then something his dad had said to him long ago came back to him: "Never focus on the *what if . . .* always focus on *the now.*" And he was right—*the now* was all that mattered.

Hunter whispered something, just loud enough for Gameknight999 to hear.

"Family takes care of family," she said, staring up at the massive spider.

"That's right," echoed Digger.

I won't focus on the what if, *I'll only focus on the* now. *And* the now *says that I have some spiders that need destroying,* Gameknight thought.

Feeling courage start to swell within his chest, the User-that-is-not-a-user glared back up at the spider queen, then moved to the outermost defensive wall. Leaping over it, he took a few steps forward, then drew his diamond sword and scratched a line in the dirt with its sharp tip.

Shaikulud, seeing this, screeched at the top of her lungs. The sound made the hundreds of spiders that surrounded them click their pointed mandibles together, creating a wave of noise that made many NPCs cover their ears . . . but Gameknight refused. Stepping forward another step, he glared up at the spider queen, then shouted with all his strength.

"BRING IT ON!"

The NPCs, hearing the User-that-is-not-a-user's voice, yelled and cheered, drowning out the clicking of the spiders. It seemed that the battle of acoustics went in favor of the NPCs. But then the spiders charged.

To Gameknight999, it seemed like everything was moving in slow motion. He could see a hundred giant spiders scurrying toward him, the little black hairs on their bodies moving about in every direction at once. They moved through the circles of light that were cast upon the battlefield by the many torches that had been placed by the NPCs. Their gray, pointed mandibles clicked together in front of their mouths as their burning red eyes all focused on him. He could hear the trickle of the river as they charged through the flowing water, sprinting toward him. The hum of the archer's bows filled his ears as the monsters splashed closer. All of these sensations seemed magnified and overwhelming until Hunter grabbed him by the shoulder and shook him.

"We must get behind the defenses," she said, then shook him again. "Gameknight! Come on."

But he was beyond thought. Gameknight had moved into that place where he just reacted, where his body did what it did best . . . and in Minecraft, that was fighting.

Ignoring his friends, Gameknight drew his other sword, and with the diamond sword in his right and his iron sword in his left, he charged at the oncoming wave of monsters, screaming at the top of his lungs, "FOR MINECRAFT!"

The villagers, seeing him with the two swords, all charged forward with him. The two armies met on the banks of the river. The NPCs hacked at the spiders as they tried to climb out of the flowing water. The villagers had dug up the blocks in the bottom of the river, increasing the depth at the banks, making it more difficult to get out. This paid off, for balls of XP were floating down the river, getting sucked into the villagers as they tore into the struggling spiders. But more eight-legged creatures flowed out of the jungle and added to their numbers. Soon there were spiders climbing over their comrades' bodies to get out of the river, the deep river bed filled in with living monsters.

The NPCs had to fall back.

Running back to their first defensive wall, the swordsmen drew their bows and fired at the spiders from ten blocks away, hoping to slow their advance. It did little good. The spiders flowed out of the river like a black flood, crashing onto the first wall as if it were not even there.

Gameknight stood at the front of the defenses, slashing at the monsters with his two swords. Spinning to the left and to the right, he was a whirlwind of death, a razor sharp tornado that moved through the Shaikulud's army with a vengeance. But for every spider he slayed, two more took its place.

They were losing.

"Fall back to the second wall!" Gameknight screamed.

The villagers, having practiced this, all disengaged from battle, turned, and sprinted through openings in the next wall. After the last villager made it through the barrier, the gaps were filled in with blocks of cobblestone.

Then Digger yelled out to the cannon tenders.

"CANNONS . . . NOW!"

His voice boomed out across the landscape, but was quickly overwhelmed by blasts of TNT.

The cannons growled and belched out their blinking cubes of TNT. The explosives lit up the night sky as they fell amongst the spiders swarming over the first wall, tearing great holes in the landscape and ripping HP from monster bodies. The archers in the towers then sent a pointed rain down upon the attackers. Gameknight could see flaming arrows from Hunter and Stitcher streak down to blocks of TNT that had been carefully hidden in that wall. They blinked for what seemed like an agonizing long time, then detonated, tearing great swaths of destruction in the spider army.

"REDSTONE . . . NOW!" Digger screamed.

Numerous levers were flipped, activating redstone circuits hidden underground. They ignited more blocks of TNT, changing the land in front of the temple into no-man's land. Spiders flew into the air as the blocks exploded, HP leaving their dark bodies as they were thrown.

But even with all this death and destruction, the spiders surged forward.

"Keep firing!" Gameknight yelled as he moved about on their last defensive wall, cheering and motivating the NPCs.

The spiders kept coming. Wave after wave kept flowing out of the dark jungle and crashing through the river. Uncertainty started to creep into Gameknight's mind.

What do I do . . . what do I do?

But before he could really think about it, he felt a tugging on his sleeve, someone shouting his name.

"Gameknight, I know what to do. Gameknight . . . TOMMY!"

He turned and found his sister standing next to him.

"I know what to do!" she shouted to her brother.

Before he could scold her for coming out of the temple, she ran to the base of the tower and yelled up at the archers.

"HUNTER . . . STITCHER . . . GET DOWN HERE NOW!"

Without waiting for a reply, she ran back to Gameknight and waited.

"What are you doing out here?" he asked. "I told you to stay in the temple!"

Monet looked at him, then raised her hand, blocky palm held outward.

"Talk to the hand," she said with a scowl.

He hated it when she said that, but knew that there was no talking to her when she was in that mood.

Hunter and Stitcher sprinted from the base of the tower and stood next to the siblings.

"What is it?" Hunter asked.

"What's wrong?" echoed Stitcher.

"Come with me," Monet said.

She turned and ran into the temple, then stopped and glared at the other three who hadn't moved.

"Follow me . . . NOW!"

The ferocity of her tone made the trio follow.

"Digger, watch our flanks and keep them fighting," Gameknight yelled to the big NPC who was now on the wall, his pickaxe slashing at the foolish spider that tried to approach. "I'll be back."

Not waiting for a reply, he sprinted after the others.

Monet led them down into the temple, deep enough where the sounds of battle were diminished.

"This will work," she said, then laid down on the ground. "All of you lay down, we have to get into the Land of Dreams."

"What?" Gameknight asked. "You know about . . ."

"Stitcher taught me," Monet answered. "She figured that since we were siblings, I'd be able to be a dream-walker like you . . . she was right. But we don't have time for a debate, so quickly . . . get into the Land of Dreams."

She put her head back and closed her eyes. Instantly, her breathing became slow and rhythmical. Gameknight laid down next to her as Hunter and Stitcher did the same.

Closing his eyes, he let himself slowly drift into that place between wakefulness and sleep, between the conscious and the unconscious . . . *to the Land of Dreams. And suddenly, the silvery fog that he'd come to know so well surrounded him. Standing nearby was Hunter, Stitcher, and Monet, each with an enchanted bow in their hands.*

Standing, Gameknight looked at his sister.

"What now?" he asked.

"Follow me . . . to the top of the temple."

She turned and sprinted up the steps, past the main entrance, and up the other flight that led them to the top floor. Using the stairs that the mason's had placed, they moved to the roof of the temple and looked out across the battlefield. They could see the partially transparent forms of the villages and spiders, locked in a dance of death as they battled in front of the temple. But Gameknight noticed a delicate purple strand of something that seemed connected to each spider, the fragile lavender threads glowing in the darkness of night.

"Watch the spider near Digger," Monet said.

Drawing an arrow back, she carefully took aim, then fired at the spider. Gameknight knew that the arrow would not hurt the spider, for the spider was not in the Land of Dreams. Besides, he could tell from the trajectory of the projectile that it was going to miss the monster completely. And sure enough, it did. Instead of striking the monster, it flew over its head and sliced the purple glowing string that was wrapped around its head. The spider, suddenly released from the grip of the purple string, looked around, then ran away, not wanting anything to do with this battle.

Monet then turned and faced her bother, a satisfied smile on her blocky face.

"I've been doing some experimenting while I was down here in the temple," she said. "We don't have to kill the spiders, we just need to cut their strings."

"This is fantastic," Hunter said as she drew back an arrow and started firing.

Stitcher moved up next to her sister and did the same, firing at the purple strands as fast as they could. Gameknight move next to his sister then imagined his favorite bow. Instantly it appeared in his hand. Drawing back the arrows that the Infinity enchantment gave him, he fired, then drew again and fired again . . . and again . . . and again.

Their barrage of dream arrows were tearing through countless purple filaments, giving those on the walls a brief respite, but Gameknight999 could see another wave of spiders coming out of the jungle. The next wave was probably three hundred strong, if not more . . . There was no way they could stand up against this wave. It was the end of them.

Gameknight noticed that the purple filaments all led back up to the sheer cliff that overlooked the temple. The silvery fog of the Land of Dreams obscured where the strands met . . . but Gameknight knew who held all the string.

And in that instant, he knew what he had to do.

"Keep firing," he said to the others.

"What are you going to do?" Hunter asked.

"Probably something stupid," he said with a smile.

"I like it already!" she replied.

Gameknight woke himself up from the Land of Dreams and stood. He could see Hunter, Stitcher, and Monet still lying on the ground, asleep, and carefully moved down the passage and up the stairs to the temple's exit.

"CRAFTER . . . WHERE'S CRAFTER?!" he yelled.

"HERE!" came a voice off to his left.

He could see Crafter battling with a cave spider, his iron sword tearing into the Brother, rending the last bit of HP from the insect's body. It disappeared with a *pop*, leaving behind three balls of XP and a ball of thread.

Turning, the NPC ran toward Gameknight999.

"Crafter, I need an ender pearl, quick," Gameknight asked.

"What?"

"Just give me an ender pearl . . . I have something that I need to do."

Reaching into his inventory, he handed the bluish sphere to Gameknight, his eyes filled with questions.

"I only have one left," Crafter said. "What are you going to do?"

"What the User-that-is-not-a-user is meant to do," he replied, then ran toward the battle lines.

Climbing to the top of the defensive wall, Gameknight looked up at the sheer cliff that overlooked the temple. Gripping the ender pearl tightly, he threw it up as high as he could. When it landed on the ground at the top of the plateau, Gameknight was instantly teleported to the same spot.

As he materialized, purple teleportation particles sparkled about him for an instant, then disappeared as pain filled his senses; you always took damage when you used an ender pearl.

Turning, he saw Shaikulud standing on the edge of the cliff, bathed in moonlight. She was looking down at her army, waving her claw-tipped arm in the air, directing her troops as if she were conducting a symphony orchestra.

"It's time for this to end!" Gameknight shouted.

The spider queen turned and looked at her enemy, then gave him a sinister fanged smile.

"So, we meet in the flesh at last," she said, her mandibles clicking excitedly. "Your actionsssss have caused me much grief, User-that-is-not-a-user. Many of my hatchlingssss had to die because of you." Her purple eyes glowed brighter, each filled with an overwhelming hatred. "I will take my revenge on you, Gameknight999, and watch you suffer, and then I will kill you."

"You can try," Gameknight growled.

Slowly, Gameknight drew his diamond sword with his right hand, then drew his iron sword with his left. Stepping forward so that he was but a few steps from the terrifying monster, he glared at Shaikulud, refusing to be afraid.

"Come on, spider . . . let's dance!"

CHAPTER 21

CUTTING THE MARIONETTE'S STRINGS

Shaikulud lunged at Gameknight999, the claws on her front legs flashing before his face, making a whistling sound as they sliced through the air. Stepping back, he brought the iron sword up to block the attack while at the same time lunging with the diamond. Her second set of legs deflected the attack as she uttered a maniacal laugh that echoed across the landscape.

"You'll have to do better than that, *user*," she screeched, her eyes now blazing.

Moving with lightning speed, she leaped at him, her claws extended. Spinning to the side, he avoided her front claws, but one from the rear gouged into his armor, causing a chunk of his diamond chest plate to fall to the ground. Gameknight looked at the armor plate and could see the jagged gouge where the spider's claw had cut through the nearly impenetrable surface.

"Apparently your armor issss not spider queen proof," Shaikulud said, laughing an eerie sinister laugh.

Gameknight charged before the monster could stop laughing, slashing at her front legs with his iron sword, spinning and attacking her side with the diamond blade. The tip tore into the spider's side, making her flash red. Pressing the attack, he continued to drive her back, both swords swinging wildly. He landed another hit with the diamond blade, then stabbed out with the iron sword, brushing against a leg.

Flash . . . red.

Shaikulud took a step back as he advanced and shot out a stream of spider's web. It caught Gameknight's foot and the end of his diamond blade. The sudden anchor on his foot almost made him fall over. Tugging violently, the User-that-is-not-a-user tried to free his foot, but it was firmly captured by the web. He pulled at his diamond sword, but it too was stuck.

Suddenly, he felt a claw rake through his armor, tearing another piece from his protective coating. Turning, he brought his iron sword up just in time to block a razor sharp claw from reaching his head. Swinging the blade wildly, he pushed the spider queen back. Gameknight knew he was stuck and had no choice; he released his grip on the hilt. With it sticking out of the white, interwoven web, he reached into his inventory and pulled out the pick. Swinging it at the web while he kept his sword at the ready, he was able to break through the web just before Shaikulud started her next attack. Rolling across the ground, he picked up his sword and the cube of spider's web just as the pointed claws streaked through the air, barely missing his head.

Drawing his diamond blade again, he turned to face the giant spider. She now had him with his back to the sheer cliff that overlooked the battle-field below. Taking a step closer, Shaikulud shot a stream of web off to the right, forming a fuzzy white wall. She then fired another stream of web to the left, completely closing off his flanks.

What is she doing? he thought.

Shooting more of the white gossamer, she placed down a wall of web directly in front of him. Moving backward, closer to the ledge, he gripped both his swords and readied himself for the next attack. Without getting ensnared, Shaikulud moved easily over the web and stepped closer to her adversary. Swinging his blades in front of him in a complicated pattern, he became a razor sharp windmill, ready to slice any part of her that came near. But she didn't attack. Instead, she threw more spiderweb around them, adding to the flanks, depositing a coating on the ground directly in front of Gameknight999.

Moving back another step or two, he noticed that she was driving him out onto a narrow strip of dirt. It stretched out over the cliff like a slender finger of soil. The sliver of land was maybe four blocks wide and extended about ten blocks out into the open air, the sides falling straight down to the ground below.

Once he was on the narrow structure, the spider queen stopped throwing her web and approached, forcing him back even farther. As she moved out onto the narrow peninsula of soil, she started to break the blocks behind her, tearing away their avenue back to the plateau . . . and safety.

"What are you doing?" Gameknight asked. "Have you come here to fight . . . or dig?"

"You will know in time, User-that-is-not-a-user," she sneered as she tore at more of the blocks.

And in that instant, Gameknight could tell what she was doing. By removing the path back to the plateau, he would be trapped with no way to get down. Looking over the edge, he could see that the river was too far away to jump into. It was easy to see that a fall from this height would be fatal . . . he was trapped.

Once she finished her excavating, Shaikulud turned and faced her enemy.

"Now it issss time for your end," the spider queen said.

"But I thought your master wants me?" Gameknight said, trying to delay the monster while he tried to think.

"Many of my hatchlingssss had to die because of you," she spat. "I watched them suffer until they disappeared in my armssss. They died because of you and those filthy NPCssss down there around the temple. You all will be destroyed."

"But your master?" the User-that-is-not-a-user replied, trying to delay her.

Reaching into the back of his mind, Gameknight looked for some idea that would let him escape this terrible creature. But there was no solution he could see, no clever trick. His only choice was to fight this monster and either win or lose.

Shaikulud attacked.

Dark spider claws tore into his diamond armor, tearing new fragments from his protective coating. She had been too fast and Gameknight had not been ready. Bringing his swords up in front of him, he swung at the beast, but he had no room to move. Taking a step toward him, Shaikulud swung at him, then diverted the attack to the ground, tearing the block at his feet out of the ground, leaving a hole that opened to the air and the ground far below. Scuttling to the side, the spider queen lunged again, this time her claw sinking into the exposed skin on his leg. Pain radiated throughout his body as if his nerves were aflame. He wanted to step back, but could feel the ledge with his square foot; he had nowhere to go.

Something his friends Kuwagata498 and Impafra had taught him long ago popped into his head: *If you don't have room to retreat, then you attack.*

So he did the only thing he could: he attacked.

Stepping forward, Gameknight swung his diamond blade in a huge sweeping arch, holding his iron sword ready for the counter-attack that would surely follow. Shaikulud deflected his blade then reached out with her dark claws, but the iron sword was there and ready. Knocking them aside, he lunged with his diamond sword, finding spider flesh. Shaikulud flashed red as she screeched out in pain. Not letting her rest, he attacked again, this time swinging with both swords. The spider queen avoided them and sprang forward, sinking two claws into his leg. At the same time, another claw raked at the armor on his arm, causing another chunk to fall off.

Agony flooded his mind as his vision blurred for just an instant. Swinging his blade in front of him, he had trouble standing. Pain was surging through his leg as if it was on fire. But just as his vision cleared, the spider queen attacked again. Wicked curved claws tore at his armor, scratching and gouging it as she landed a flurry of attacks. Gameknight tried to keep his swords up in front of him, but the claws seemed to be everywhere at once. A claw found exposed skin and he screamed as pain spread throughout his body.

"Do not fear, User-that-is-not-a-user, your suffering issss almost over," Shaikulud said with a sneer.

Gameknight looked up at the monster, then turned and looked down at the temple defenders. He could see that they were losing; the number of spiders was just too great. Suddenly, he saw a group of cavalry charge into the mass of insects, swords carving a pathway through the monsters. At the front was Digger . . . with Monet riding right behind him!

"Ahh . . . I see some of your NPCssss are trying to run away," Shaikulud said, her mandibles clicking in anticipation of his death. "It issss no matter. There issss another massive army of zombiessss on the way . . . a gift from the Maker. They will not get far."

She stepped a little closer and glared down at him with those terrible purple eyes.

"You have caused great problemssss in Minecraft, and many monsterssss have suffered because of you."

"What you are doing here is wrong," Gameknight said, trying to delay the inevitable. "Spiders can live in peace with NPCs."

"NO," she snapped. "Spiderssss and NPCssss are just too different. We have nothing in common. NPCssss live in those ridiculoussss wooden boxessss instead of living in a cave where it issss warm and dry. They feed on innocent animalssss instead of eating plantssss as we do. They only have two legssss and are alwayssss on the verge of falling down. There is nothing in common between our two peoplessss."

"Yes there is," Gameknight said as part of the solution materialized in his mind. "You both care about your young. NPCs cherish their young; they are the most important thing to them, as your hatchlings are to you."

Gameknight could see this thought percolate in the spider's mind, the blazing hatred in her purple eyes fading a bit.

"Our children and your hatchlings are the common thread that binds us together. And where there is one thing in common, there will be more. We just have to *want* to find the similarities."

A peculiar thunking sound started to float up from the ground below, slowly growing louder and louder.

"You use your wordsssss as well as you use your bladessss," the spider queen said. "But you are just trying to avoid your death. NPCsssss cannot be trusted and userssss like you are even worse. The spider race has suffered at the handsssss of the two-legs long enough. I do not care what the Maker wantssss with you, it is time for you to die."

Moving closer, Shaikulud reared up on her back two legs and extended six claws toward the User-that-is-not-a-user. Stiffening every muscle, the spider queen readied herself for the final attack. Gameknight looked up at the massive creature and was filled with fear. He knew that he was beaten and his body was just giving up. But then the thunking sound grew louder and louder. Turning his head toward the sound, he saw Digger building a column of dirt straight up into the air, jumping up, then placing the block beneath him. Holding onto his back was his sister, Monet113.

"Get ready for your end," Shaikulud said with a sneer.

Gameknight brought up his swords, but knew that they would not be able to stave off this last attack.

Shaikulud's massive body slowly descended down upon him, moving in slow motion as his mind watched the scene unfold like it were some kind of movie. Her pointed claws sparkled in the moonlight as her hateful eyes cast a purple glow on the surroundings. But suddenly, an enchanted flaming arrow streaked through the air and hit the spider queen in the head, knocking her off balance. She flashed over and over as the headshot tore into her HP. The massive body continued to fall toward Gameknight999, but instead of looking like a dark fuzzy wall of pain descending upon him, it looked like a flashing red blanket. Shaikulud flashed faster and faster as she fell until . . .

The monster's body disappeared just before landing on Gameknight999, covering him with silk thread and probably a hundred balls of XP.

Shaikulud, the queen of the spiders, was dead.

CHAPTER 22

A SINGLE ARROW

A cheer rang out from around the temple. Turning his head, Gameknight looked down at the NPC defenders. All of the spiders had stopped their assault, taking a step back. The dark beasts looked around at the NPCs and then each other, confused. One spider turned and ran away, then another and another until it became an avalanche of retreating monsters, their black bodies disappearing into the jungle.

The fighting had stopped.

Suddenly, the sound of breaking glass filled Gameknight's ears as he felt coated in some kind of liquid. Looking back toward his sister, he saw that she had a bottle of something purple in her hand. Throwing it, the splash potion hit the block on which he lay and shattered, bathing him in a healing potion that instantly recharged his HP. Pain faded from his body as the magical potion restored his body back to full strength. Standing, he looked at his sister and smiled, his eyes filled with gratitude.

"What good can one arrow be?" she said with a smile. "Wasn't that what you said to me."

Gameknight looked at the ground, embarrassed that he'd misjudged her, but then looked back to his sister when she started to laugh.

Using more blocks of dirt, Digger carefully built a narrow bridge so that he and Monet could move to the plateau. With his sword, the big NPC smashed through the blocks of spiderweb, carving a path to Gameknight's position. Stepping up to the edge of the cliff, he carefully placed blocks of dirt so that Gameknight could also move off the precipice and back to safety.

Standing and testing his newly healed legs, Gameknight999 carefully walked across the narrow dirt bridge and moved to his sister's side. Wrapping his arms around her small body, he gave her a gigantic hug.

"You're amazing," he said to Monet, then turned to look at Digger. "Both of you."

Gameknight reached over and placed his hand on Digger's shoulder.

"It was her idea," Digger said in a deep voice.

"I could see you in the Land of Dreams and could tell that you needed some help," she explained.

"Well, I'm pretty glad you ignored my instructions and left the temple," Gameknight said. "That was quite a shot."

Monet113 beamed with pride.

Moving to the edge of the cliff, Gameknight looked down on the temple. He could see many of the NPCs were leaving their defensive walls to pursue the spiders, but none of the eight-legged creatures stopped to fight. They all seemed intent on leaving the area as quickly as possible, each monster running off in a different direction. Most of the NPCs followed them to the edge of the clearing then stopped; no one wanting to risk the dangers of the jungle at night.

Slowly, Gameknight saw a lone figure emerge from the dark entrance . . . the Oracle. She moved carefully down the steps, leaning heavily on her cane and standing before the ancient structure, her gray hair standing out against the shadowy background. Looking up to the sheer cliff, she gave Gameknight999 a smile as she waved. Gameknight was about to wave back when suddenly another presence materialized in front of the old woman. It looked to be an NPC, but there was something strange about his face, as if there were something hidden behind those dark eyes. They flared bright and sinister.

Herobrine had finally arrived.

"So you finally left the safety of your temple, old woman," Herobrine screamed at the Oracle, his words carrying across the clearing and up to the plateau.

He disappeared and reappeared behind the Oracle, placing himself between the old woman and the entrance to the Temple, blocking off any chance for her to escape back into the cobblestone structure.

"I wondered when you would show up," the Oracle said with a sneer as she turned to face him. "Clearly you had a hand in this war."

Herobrine smiled.

"Many NPCs and spiders had to die today because of you," she said.

Herobrine's smile grew even bigger, his eyes glowing bright white.

"But as you can see, your attempt to destroy these people failed," the Oracle said. "The User-that-is-not-you-user has stopped the carnage and defeated your plans. He stopped all the killing and brought us peace."

"You are mistaken," Herobrine growled.

"Oh?"

"Yes," he answered. "The killing is not quite finished."

Gameknight could see Herobrine draw his diamond sword and swing it toward the Oracle. Bringing her cane up, she was just barely able to block the attack, but clearly she did not have to skill to fight him in mortal combat.

"Nooooo!" Gameknight shouted.

Moving to the edge of the cliff, he could see the ground far, far below. No amount of HP could sustain that fall, but he knew he had no choice. Glancing over his shoulder, he looked at his sister for what he figured would be the last time in his life, then jumped off the cliff, his sister's screams echoing in his ears as he fell.

As he fell, Gameknight locked eyes with his sister. She had a look of terror painted on her square face. Gameknight, however, had a smile on his face and a look of pride in his eyes for his sister. Her impulsive *act now, think later* attitude had likely saved his life. And at that moment, as he fell below the plateau and she disappeared from sight, he never felt closer to his sister, Jenny.

He looked down at the ground and saw it coming up at him. Reaching into his inventory, he prepared to hit the ground. Gameknight999 knew that if he timed this wrong, he had no shot at survival. He had to get it right . . . or perish.

The air rushed past his ears as he fell, roaring like a tornado. He knew that this fall would only take a few seconds, but things seemed to move in slow motion as his brain took in the terrifying scene.

If only the river had been closer. He could have jumped into it and easily survived the fall, but it was another ten blocks away . . . it didn't matter. The safety of the blue water was out of his reach.

Here it comes, he thought, fear and panic starting to fill his mind.

Wrapping his fingers around the fuzzy cube in his inventory, he got ready.

Here it comes . . . almost there . . . and . . . NOW!

Pulling out the cube of spiderweb, he placed it on the ground just before he hit. As soon as his feet touched the web, he instantly slowed down and sank into the sticky filaments. Waiting until he settled to the ground, Gameknight pulled out his sword and chopped through the gossamer strands. With two hits, the spiderweb disappeared, freeing his legs.

He'd survived.

Looking up at the cliff top, he could see Digger and Monet looking down at him, smiles gradually replacing the shock on their faces. Giving them a satisfied smile, he waved then turned and faced the temple. Herobrine had his sword out and was chopping away at the Oracle, her cane flashing here and there to stop the attacks, but just barely. He could see that the old woman was no match for Herobrine, and that the vile shadow-crafter was just toying with his prey.

But as he watched the battle, he could remember what it had been like fighting that monster in front of Crafter's village. Fear started to surge through his body as he relived that terrible encounter in his mind.

Can I face him again? he thought. *Do I have what's needed to stand up to him?*

The fear slowly morphed into panic as he watched the battle before him, uncertainty spreading through him like a virus. For the briefest of moments, Gameknight999 considered running away, but knew that if he ran, if he could have helped someone in need but chose cowardice instead . . . that decision would haunt him for the rest of his life.

No, fleeing was not an option. So, with terror filling every fiber of his being, he gripped the hilt of his diamond sword and sprinted toward his enemy, Herobrine.

CHAPTER 23

HEROBRINE

Herobrine hadn't noticed him yet. He was still slashing at the Oracle, driving her backward with each attack. The old woman's cane was deflecting most of the attacks but some of them were getting through. Flashing red when the diamond blade reached her flesh, Gameknight could see her grimace, her face a visage of pain and fear.

Another attack landed, Herobrine's blade cutting into her shoulder. The Oracle shouted out in pain as Gameknight waded through the river and sprinted toward the battling pair.

"Your time is at an end, Oracle," Herobrine shouted, his eyes burning bright. "All I needed was that fool, Gameknight999, to draw you out of your cowardly temple." He leaned closer to the old woman and laughed. "It is now time for you to be deleted."

Gameknight could see the Oracle look up at her foe and a look of resignation came across her face; she knew she was about to perish. Sprinting, the User-that-is-not-a-user ran as fast as he could to get to her, but he wasn't sure if he'd make it in time. As he ran, Herobrine slowly raised his sword and prepared for the killing blow. He then swung his blade down at the Oracle.

But when it was within just a hair's breadth of the old NPC, Gameknight smashed into Oracle and knocked her to the side, bringing his own blade up just in time to met his enemy's. Herobrine's sword crashed down onto Gameknight's blade with the force of an iron golem's steel-fisted strike. His arm almost went numb as it absorbed the blow, but his strength held as he pushed away the violent attack. Looking up at his enemy, Gameknight saw a look of surprise on Herobrine's face, his eyes dimming. Spinning, he faked an attack with his sword, then shot out a kick to Herobrine's stomach that pushed him back a few steps.

Glaring at the User-that-is-not-a-user, Hero-brine screamed a frustrated, blood thirsty scream that resonated all across the land, making the very fabric of Minecraft cringe in fear.

Gameknight999 smiled.

"You interrupted me!" Herobrine wailed. "I'd been waiting to destroy that old hag for a century . . . AND YOU INTERRUPTED ME!

Gameknight smiled again.

"Too bad . . . so sad," the User-that-is-not-a-user mocked.

Herobrine stepped back and glared at Game-knight999, his hate-filled eyes flaring like two intense suns.

"You've meddled in my plans for the last time," he growled.

Gameknight was about to say something sarcastic back to his adversary, but at that moment Herobrine charged. His evil diamond sword was like a flash of blue lightning as it streaked toward Gameknight's head. Bringing his own sword up just in time, the User-that-is-not-a-user deflected the blow. Spinning to the side, Gameknight sliced at Herobrine, hoping to catch him by surprise . . . but he was not there.

Pain suddenly exploded in his side and Herobrine's sword found flesh.

"Ha, ha, ha," his enemy cackled. "When will you learn? User-that-is-not-a-user, I cannot be defeated. I can disappear, then appear right behind you in the blink of an eye. I can attack two places at once, and you cannot stop me."

He laughed a maniacal, evil laugh that made little square goose-bumps form on his arms and neck.

"Use the weapon!" a voice yelled from the edge of the jungle.

Glancing in that direction, he could see Hunter's red hair standing out against the dark green foliage.

No, it doesn't feel right, he thought to himself. *I have to use it at the right time . . . but how will I know? What if I use it wrong?*

"Today, you either take the Gateway of Light back to the physical world to save your miserable life . . . or you die!"

Herobrine disappeared, then materialized with his sword bearing down on him. Just as Gameknight brought his sword up, Herobrine teleported to his other side, slashing into the User-that-is-not-a-user's armor. Another chunk of the diamond coating fell to the ground, allowing his enemy's blade to again find flesh.

He flashed red.

Gameknight tried to ignore the pain while he spun and slashed at Herobrine . . . but again he was somewhere else. Stepping back, the User-that-is-not-a-user growled as frustration and fear began to fill his mind.

How can I defeat him? Gameknight thought. He then reached out, through the music of Minecraft and to his friend. *Shawny . . . are you there?*

Yep, came the answer, Shawny's text filling his mind.

What about the dig . . . Gameknight thought to his friend, but was interrupted

It's still smoking, Shawny said. *I think I found the components that fried, but I'm having trouble finding the right replacements!*

Gameknight sighed.

I hate this! he thought to himself. *I don't want to be the User-that-is-not-a-user, I just want to be a kid. This responsibility is too much.*

Gameknight then slouched a bit as the feeling of defeat started to fill his soul. And then that strange mystical voice filled his mind again.

You can accomplish only what you can imagine, the voice said. *Put aside your uncertainty and accept who you are and what you can do. Fear is a mask that hides the possible from your eyes. Be the User-that-is-not-a-user!*

The words tried to chip away at his fear, but they were unsuccessful . . . he was terrified. Taking a step back, he glared at Herobrine, but knew that fear was painted across his face.

"I can see that you are contemplating using the Gateway . . . take your time and think it through," Herobrine said. "When you are about to take your last breath, I know you'll run and try to escape death . . . it is inevitable."

He then gave Gameknight999 an eerie toothy smile.

I hate this! he thought. *I hate being afraid of him.*

But then Gameknight thought about those words. With all of his mental strength, he imagined what it would be like to not be afraid, then imagined that he could handle this responsibility. He thought about it hard and drove the images through the mask of his fear and into his mind . . . and it began to feel somehow . . . real.

Standing up straight, the User-that-is-not-a-user stared across at Herobrine. A guttural, animal-like growl grew in Gameknight's throat and flowed out across the landscape.

I won't be afraid! he thought. *I can do this . . . I CHOOSE not to be afraid.*

Glancing about the landscape, he could see all eyes were locked on him, his sister and Digger watching from the sheer cliff.

"NO MORE!" Gameknight yelled as he took a step forward, the thought of him conquering his own fear shining bright in his mind.

Herobrine smiled, but it seemed a little forced, his eyes dimming just the faintest bit.

"NO MORE!" the User-that-is-not-a-user said again as he brought his sword up in front of him.

Herobrine glared at his foe, his smile starting to fade.

"NO MORE! I won't be afraid of you anymore!" Gameknight shouted. He was fully imagining overcoming his fear and facing this monster. It was possible, he knew that it was.

And then Gameknight999, the User-that-is-not-a-user, charged.

CHAPTER 24

GAMEKNIGHT999 FIGHTS BACK

Gameknight's sword streaked toward Herobrine, slicing through the air so quickly that the razor sharp edge made a subtle whistling sound. The diamond swords smashed together with such ferocity that sparks shot out, small chips of diamond raining down on the two combatants. As Gameknight had expected, Herobrine disappeared, then reappeared behind him, but this time he was ready. Drawing his iron sword, he held it over his shoulder so that it protected his back. Another smash sounded as Herobrine's diamond blade crashed into Gameknight's iron.

Spinning, Gameknight attacked with the two swords, slashing up high while at the same time stabbing down low. Herobrine moved with lightning sped, flashing to one side, then to the other, but always he was met by one of Gameknight's blades. The battle raged, first Herobrine on the attack, then Gameknight. They danced across the landscape, trying to catch the other off guard, but it was an equal match . . . except for one thing.

Gameknight was getting tired.

Herobrine charged again and again, his diamond blade slashing at him from all sides. He was blocking the attacks, but just barely.

SLASH . . . pain erupted in Gameknight's arm.

He blocked another attack and spun to slash at Herobrine, but the monster was too fast.

STAB . . . his back exploded in agony.

Rolling to the side, Gameknight brought his swords around, ready for the next attack, but he was starting to slow, fatigue making his arms and legs feel heavy.

CRASH . . . another chunk of armor fell to the ground.

Gameknight jumped backward, then charged at his evil adversary. He refused to retreat.

SLICE . . . the sting of Herobrine's blade lit up his side.

I'm losing, he thought, and the image of his victory against Herobrine slowly faded from his mind as it was replaced by fear. *He's just too fast . . . I can't do it.*

Herobrine attacked again, charging straight at him. His diamond sword streaked straight toward Gameknight's helmeted head. The User-that-is-not-a-user blocked the attack, but was suddenly knocked off his feet by a savage kick to his stomach. As he fell backward, his eyes glanced up at Monet113. He could hear her yelling "noooo!" as he fell and hit the ground.

And then Herobrine was standing over him, one foot on his right arm, the other on his left. The monster stared down at him with his glowing hate-filled eyes, a malicious self-satisfied grin on his square face.

He was trapped.

"Use it!" screamed Hunter.

But he couldn't, his hands were pinned to the ground, unable to reach into his inventory. Gameknight could feel Herobrine's glowing eyes staring down at him, but he refused to look back. Instead, he looked up at the plateau. His sister stared down at him, a look of terror painted on her boxy face. Looking back at his enemy, Gameknight could see Herobrine turn his face up toward the plateau, then turn back to his fallen enemy.

"Ahh . . . I see there is another one like you," Herobrine said, his voice filled with venomous glee. "This changes everything. If you refuse to take the Gateway of Light, then I will dispose of you and use the young girl. I'm sure she will be more easily subdued than you."

Herobrine leaned down a little and glared into Gameknight's eyes.

"Choose . . . take the Gateway or die!"

Gameknight looked up at his enemy, but shook his head.

Even if I could use the digitizer to get home, I wouldn't, he thought.

Herobrine sighed.

"As you wish," Herobrine said. "Say goodbye, User-that-is-not-a-user."

And as Gameknight999 saw Herobrine raise his diamond sword and prepare for the final attack, he thought he heard something that sounded like thunder in the distance. It was a strange sort of thunder, like a grumbling storm approaching from somewhere far, far away. And as Herobrine's blade started to fall, moving in slow motion, Gameknight999 closed his eyes and waited for the end.

CHAPTER 25

GROWLING THUNDER

Suddenly, the rumbling sound turned into a howling hurricane. Gameknight glanced at the temple opening and saw what must have been a hundred wolves running right toward him, Herder at the tip of the furry spear.

Herobrine stopped his attack when he heard the sound. Gameknight saw him look down at his helpless victim, then back at the charging animals.

"Another time, User-that-is-not-a-user," the vile shadow-crafter said, then disappeared just as the wave of snapping jaws flowed over Gameknight999.

Soft padded paws ran over his body as the wolves pursued Herobrine, their growls filling their air. A pair of skinny hands reached down and grabbed Gameknight by the arm, then lifted him up. Gameknight found Herder looking at him with a worried look on his face.

"Are you alright?" Herder asked.

"Yes, thanks to you and your friends," Gameknight replied.

The massive wave of wolves continued to surge out of the temple, flowing around Gameknight and

Herder as if they were a large stone in the middle of a river. The wolves shot out in all directions, looking for their prey, Herobrine. They moved across the landscape with incredible speed, their white furry bodies moving past NPCs without a thought as they shot into the jungle.

In the distance, Gameknight saw Herobrine materialize at the top of a tall junglewood tree, his eyes burning bright. He pointed at the User-that-is-not-a-user with his diamond sword, then also pointed at Monet113.

"We will meet again," Herobrine yelled, his voice just barely audible over the growling wolves. The animals instantly turned and headed straight toward the tree, their eyes burning bright red. "But next time, things will be different. I'm done underestimating you, Gameknight999. When we meet again, I will destroy you, then force your little friend to take the Gateway of Light. My escape from this prison will happen with or without your help."

And then he disappeared, his glowing, hate-filled eyes that last thing to fade from sight.

With their prey gone, the wolves returned back to the temple, flowing around the entrance for a moment, then obediently sitting on the ground near the Oracle. The NPCs also moved toward the temple entrance, their weapons still in their hands. Gameknight could see some villagers constructing a pool of water at the foot of the cliff, then saw Digger and Monet jump off the plateau and land in the cushioning pond.

"Why didn't you use the weapon?" Hunter asked as she approached, her enchanted bow shimmering in her hand.

Gameknight shook his head.

"It didn't feel like the right time," he answered.

"You mean when he had you on your back and was about to kill you . . . that didn't seem like the right time?" she asked.

He shook his head again.

"No, that wasn't the time," Gameknight answered.

"You are quite the patient user," Crafter said as he moved to his friend's side. "I thought Herobrine was going to kill you."

"So did I."

"And yet you still did not use the weapon," Crafter said.

Gameknight turned and looked at the Oracle, who stood by the temple entrance.

"She said that I would know when it was the right time," Gameknight said. "Well, I wasn't sure, so I figured that it wasn't the right time."

The Oracle nodded her boxy head, her gray hair moving back and forth like a silvery wave.

"The User-that-is-not-a-user is wise," she said in a scratchy voice.

"So what now?" Stitcher asked as she approached, her eyes looking at the dark jungle suspiciously.

Suddenly a pair of arms wrapped around Gameknight's body as Monet dove into him, laughing with glee while at the same time crying with relief. Gameknight hugged her back for a long moment, then released her.

She looked up at her brother, then punched him in the arm.

"You scared me when you jumped off that cliff," she chided. "What were you thinking?"

"Well, I had to get down here to protect the Oracle," Gameknight answered. "That was the only way I could get to her quickly."

"Where did you get the block of spider's web?" Crafter asked.

Gameknight reached into his inventory and pulled out the enchanted pickaxe.

"I took this out of the chest in the temple," that User-that-is-not-a-user explained. "It must have the *Silk Touch* enchantment on it."

He turned and looked at the Oracle. She smiled and nodded.

"How did you know that I'd need that?" Gameknight asked.

She just shrugged.

"It is my job to know what is necessary," she replied.

"Well, you could have told him that he'd need to fight the spider queen and would need some spider's web," Hunter said, her voice edged with frustration.

"Too much information would cause the User-that-is-not-a-user to make different decisions," the Oracle said. "I cannot see what *will* happen, I can only see what *might* happen."

"You speak in riddles," Hunter snapped. "Why don't you just tell us what to do!"

"As you wish, Hunter," the Oracle answered. "You should decide what you are going to do, for there is a massive army of zombies on their way here as we speak."

The NPCs all glanced at each other nervously, then turned and faced the jungle, many drawing their weapons.

"Be at peace for now," the Oracle explained. "The sun will rise before they reach here. You may be safe, but many have learned that wearing a hat will protect them from the sun. The zombies will be equipped to battle during the day. It would be important to come to a decision as to what your next step will be as soon as possible."

Gameknight looked at Crafter, then looked at the NPCs around him. He could see items littered all across the landscape; armor, weapons and other items floating about just off the ground. Many had died this day protecting Minecraft. They couldn't fight another battle right now.

"We have to get out of here, somehow," Gameknight said.

Crafter nodded.

"But how?" Digger asked. "The extreme hills ring this place. We cannot climb them. The only way out is back through the jungle."

"And the zombie army will likely be waiting for us," Stitcher added.

Gameknight looked out at the jungle, lost in thought. He was waiting for some idea, some brilliant and clever solution to appear in his mind, but there was nothing . . . only silence. But then a voice echoed within his brain, a familiar voice . . . Shawny.

Look behind the temple, his friend said.

"What?" Gameknight asked aloud.

The NPCs looked at him as if he were crazy.

Look behind the temple, Shawny said. *What don't you understand? Sometimes I think you are so dense and . . .*

Nevermind! he snapped.

"Someone look behind the temple," Gameknight ordered.

Two villagers ran behind the ancient structure, then returned in seconds.

"There are a bunch of chests back there," the Woodcutter said, his red smock standing out against the gray stone of the temple. "They're filled with boats . . . hundreds of them."

"Boats?" Hunter asked. "How are we going to battle an army of zombies with boats?"

"We aren't," Gameknight answered. "We're going to escape. This is all part of Herobrine's plan. He thinks that we're trapped here and he's hoping that the zombies will destroy most of us and probably destroy the wolves as well so that he can return. Well, we won't play his game. We're going to disappear again and then face him in a place of our choosing." Gameknight then reached out and placed a hand on Hunter's shoulder. "The battle for Minecraft is not over . . . it is just beginning."

"The User-that-is-not-a-user grows wise," the Oracle said, her voice resonating with wisdom and age.

"Quickly, we need to dismantle our defenses and then get to the boats," Gameknight999 ordered.

"But where will we go?" someone asked.

"Away from here," Monet said.

Gameknight nodded his head, then pulled out his pick and started taking apart the defensive structures they'd built, the rest of the NPCs joining in.

Monet moved to his side and spoke in a low voice.

"Tommy, do you know what you are doing?" she asked.

He scowled at his sister.

"Sorry . . . Gameknight999, do you know what you are doing, where we have to go?"

"No," he whispered, "but anywhere is better than staying here."

"Do you have a plan?" she asked.

The only plan he'd formulated was to run away. He thought about sailing across the ocean and arriving at some new land. But then suddenly the puzzle pieces started tumbling around in his head, and one of them landed in place.

A village . . . of course, he thought.

And then the other pieces started to fall home, the plan slowly coming together in his head.

Minecarts . . . and traps . . . big traps, he thought.

And as the rest of the pieces fell into place in his mind, Gameknight smiled.

CHAPTER 26

TO THE SEA

The boats slowly moved out across the ocean, first in pairs, then in large groups. Each held a lone NPC, for that was all that would fit in the boat . . . one person. Gameknight stood on the shore and watched the boats head off into the distance, all of them continuing their journey to the east.

"Come on," Stitcher said to Gameknight.

"Not until everyone gets in a boat," he answered. "I won't leave anyone behind."

She shrugged, then jumped into one of the small wooden vessels. Pushing off from the shoreline, her boat slowly moved across the water, heading out into the open ocean.

Just then, Smithy was walking by with Herder draped over his shoulders.

"I can't leave them behind," the lanky boy complained, flailing his arms and legs. "They are my friends."

"You know they can't go into the boats," Smithy said to the boy. "And if you stay here, the zombie army will get you. The only way is for you to leave with the others, then the animals will just go off into the jungle and live out their lives in safety."

"But . . ."

Smithy ignored the boy's complaints and dropped him in the boat, then gave it a shove so that it moved away from the shore.

"My friends . . . my friends," Herder cried, but continued heading to the east.

Smithy then turned to Gameknight.

"Thank you," the User-that-is-not-a-user said to the big NPC. "I know that was not very easy."

"Pffft . . . he's light," Smithy said as he jumped into a boat. "See you on the other side of the ocean."

Pushing off, the blacksmith headed off to the east, following the other NPCs.

"This is a good plan," a voice said next to him, "you know, sailing away across an unknown ocean to some unknown land . . . really a great idea."

Turning, Gameknight found Hunter standing at his side, her red hair almost glowing in the light of the rising sun. A moaning sound trickled out of the jungle behind them. Instinctively, she drew her bow and notched an arrow. Gameknight could see that familiar look in her eye; the desire to punish the monsters for what they had done to her family. It still worried him . . . would she ever accept that violence was not the only answer . . . would she ever be at peace?

"You need to get into a boat," Gameknight said as he put a gentle hand on her bow and pointed it to the ground. "We can't stay and fight."

"But it's just a few hundred," she complained. "I could go out and have some fun for a while, then catch up with you."

"You know that if we get separated out there on the ocean, we'll never find each other. Besides, the time for fighting is over . . . it's time to run and save the lives of those around us. Fighting isn't always the answer."

"With monsters it is," Hunter relied. "They're too different from us. The zombies in their weird zombie-towns, and the spiders with those bizarre purple threads connecting them together . . . they're strange, and we'll never be at peace with them. All of the monsters should just be exterminated."

"Hunter, you know that's not true," another voice said from behind them.

Monet113 walked up and stood between her brother and Hunter.

"We don't *need* to kill the zombies," Monet said. "We just need to understand them . . . and they need to understand us. Then we can have peace."

"Understand zombies . . . ha! You might as well ask a pig to fly," Hunter replied. "It will never happen . . . we have nothing in common, other than a desire to destroy each other."

Another moan floated out of the dense jungle, causing Hunter to raise her bow again.

"Hunter, get in a boat, we aren't staying and we aren't going to wait for you," Gameknight999 said. "This is all part of Herobrine's plans. We aren't going to let him decide where the next battle will be . . . now GO!"

Monet grabbed Hunter by the hand and led her to the shore, then gently shoved her into a boat. With her glaring over her shoulder, Hunter's boat moved off to the east, following the others. Once she was sure that the NPC wasn't going to turn around, Monet returned to Gameknight's side.

"You know," Gameknight said to his sister. "I was really proud of what you did back there during the battle."

"I didn't do anything special," she said.

"Yes you did!" he snapped. "You showed me how to stop the spider queen's control over the other spiders. And you ignored my instructions at the right time and came out to save me with your *one* arrow."

Monet113 smiled, a pink blush forming on her square cheeks.

"If it hadn't been for you, we would have likely lost that battle," Gameknight said. "You saw what you needed to do and you did it. I have to always calculate what will happen, and plan on contingencies and back-up plans, but you can just act." He put his arm around his sister's blocky shoulders. "I really envy that you can do that."

"Really?"

He nodded his head.

"Even though your impulsiveness gets you in a lot of trouble too," Gameknight added, "and it seems that I'm the one that has to get you out of it."

"Like here, in Minecraft?" she asked.

The User-that-is-not-a-user nodded.

Monet wrapped her arm around her brother and gave him a slight squeeze.

"You think you can't just act," she said, "but when you figured out that the spider queen was the key, you just ran out there and attacked there . . . like a crazy guy."

"Yeah . . . but . . ."

"And when you saw the Oracle was in trouble, you charged straight toward Herobrine," Monet said. "That wasn't the safest thing to do either."

"Well," he thought about his two friends, Impafra and Kuwagata498, "when you have no choice and can't retreat, you attack."

"You always do that, make excuses for your bravery," Monet chided. "This community of NPCs will follow you to the end of the world if necessary because they have faith in you, as do I." She then held her hand out, gesturing to all the boats that were moving off across the ocean. "Look what you've done here. You've snatched everyone from the jaws of defeat and escaped Herobrine's trap. Those zombies are going to come out of the jungle at sunset and find everyone gone. You're a hero!"

"Well . . . I don't know . . . I mean, I still have to figure out how to use this . . ."

"You're going to figure out that weapon-thing, I know it, so don't worry. And then Herobrine will be sorry he ever tangled with the User-that-is-not-a-user." She paused and looked up at him. "I'm glad you're my big brother."

And before he could say anything, she jumped into a boat and move off across the ocean, leaving Gameknight standing on the shoreline. Looking around, he could see that all the other villagers had left, and for the first time in a long time, he felt proud of himself.

Maybe I can handle this responsibility . . . being the User-that-is-not-a-user, he thought. *I can't be the hero that these NPCs need if I don't imagine myself in that role. And I think now, I can see myself being that person.*

"The User-that-is-not-a-user is beginning to understand," said a scratchy voice from behind.

Turning, he saw the Oracle walking toward him. The old woman moved slowly, painfully, through the jungle, her wooden cane helping her to walk. It clicked when it found purchase on a rocky block or the occasional cube of sandstone.

"What do you mean . . . I'm beginning to understand?"

"Handling responsibility is a skill like any other. It takes practice, but more importantly, it takes faith in yourself to know how and when to do the right thing," the old woman explained. "Sometimes, it is the heaviest of burdens when you have to make a difficult choice, and sometimes it is the greatest of joys. In either case, it takes character and faith in one's self to handle the responsibility that has been thrust upon you. And I see you learning to have faith in yourself and your friends . . . especially your sister, for you cannot do all this by yourself. A wise leader uses the strengths of the people around him."

She moved to his side and looked at him, her eyes boring straight into his.

"But what if I can't figure it out?" Gameknight said as he pulled out the weapon. Its pink surface seemed to glow in the light of morning. "Everyone is counting on me, but I don't know what to do."

"You still have much to learn," she said as she shook her head. "Have faith in yourself and in those around you, for help will come to you from the most unexpected of places." The Oracle then placed a wrinkled hand on his shoulder. She then spoke in a low voice as if uttering the secret to some sacred mystery. "Look to the lowliest and most insignificant of creatures, for that is where your salvation will lie."

"What?"

But she did not answer. Instead, the Oracle turned and started walking back to the temple.

"Come on, I need to get you into a boat," Game-knight said.

The old woman shook her head, her gray hair waving back and forth.

"No, my place is here," she said, glancing over her shoulder.

"But the zombies, they'll . . ."

"They cannot harm me," she responded.

"But what about Herobrine . . . won't he return?"

"Most certainly."

"Aren't you afraid of him?" he asked.

She stopped and turned to face Gameknight999.

"Herobrine is but a spoiled child who will never be satisfied with what he has." She took a step closer. "He cannot harm me just as he cannot harm you."

"But I can't defeat him in battle . . . he's too fast."

"Then don't battle him . . . or at least don't fight him the way he wants. He can be defeated; you just have to figure out how. And to do that, you'll need wisdom and strength."

"You mean I have to get stronger?"

"No," she replied. "You only need strength of character and courage to do what is necessary."

"But what about the weapon you gave me, how do I . . ."

"It is the same with the weapon. You need character and wisdom to know how to use it, and more importantly, when." The Oracle took two slow, methodical steps back to Gameknight, then leaned close so that their blocky heads were almost touching. Moving her lips so that they nearly brushed his ear, she whispered in a scratchy voice. "You already know what the weapon is, you just haven't opened your mind to the possibility yet. The wisdom, courage, and character, that is what's needed . . . the User-that-is-not-a-user already possesses these traits. You just don't realize it . . . yet. Hopefully, at the critical moment, when everything hangs by the thinnest of threads, you will come to understand your potential and do what is needed . . . everything depends on it."

"But what about . . ."

"No more questions," the Oracle said as she took a step back. "You should listen to your sister and bask in this victory. You defeated the spiders and now are escaping from Herobrine's trap so that you can fight another day. The User-that-is-not-a-user is truly the one who will save Minecraft."

The old woman then put her fist to her chest in salute, then turned and slowly moved back to her temple.

As he watched her go, Gameknight thought about everything that had happened. He'd done what his dad had told him to do . . . take care of his sister. She was still safe, even though she was still stuck here in Minecraft. He'd also take care of all the NPCs . . . no . . . his Minecraft family. Many had perished, and he felt responsible for every life that was lost, but he had done his best, and for that, Gameknight999 felt good.

Maybe I can handle this responsibility, he thought. *Maybe the secret to being responsible for others is just doing your best and never giving up. That's what Dad is doing . . . trying to sell his inventions to take care of his family. But I wish he were home, I could really use his help right now.*

Climbing into the boat, he shoved off from the shore and followed the other boats. In the distance, he saw a rocket streak into the sky then explode high overhead, forming a giant sparkling display of light. Some of the boats on the edge of the formation turned slightly to aim for that rocket. Crafter was using them to keep the boats together and on the same course. He always knew what to do.

"Look to the lowliest and most insignificant of creatures, for that is where your salvation will lie."

Looking back over his shoulder, Gameknight could see the Oracle looking out of a window on the top floor of the temple. He waved, her riddle echoing in his head, then turned and headed toward the fireworks in the distance. And as he looked at the fleet of boats before him, he realized that these were all the lives that he'd saved . . . his friends . . . his family. And for the first time in a long time, Gameknight999, the User-that-is-not-a-user, relaxed.

THE JUNGLE TEMPLE ORACLE SEEDS

had a really fun time choosing some cool and exotic settings to send Gameknight999 and company to throughout this book. Below, I've listed some seeds that you can enter into Minecraft so that you can actually see the landscape described in the story! These seeds will definitely work with Minecraft 1.8, but you'll have to check to see if the edition of the game you're playing on supports seeds.

If you need a primer on seeds, a quick search on YouTube should give you what you need! You'll find countless tutorials on the subject.

Chapter 3
    Villager seed: -770290065

Chapter 4
    Roofed Forest Biome seed: 426309126

Chapter 5
    Desert village: 1264417242569508166
    (Note the desert temple that is partially buried right near the village.)

Chapter 7
Birch Forest biome: -9101136179474925827

Chapter 7
Ice Spikes biome: -1603209754400422622

Chapter 8
Extreme Hills Biome seed: -6113936998497547891

Chapter 11
Stronghold, directly under the blacksmith's shop: 5886950453418879987

Chapter 15
Jungle seed: 1977385972517642323
This is a massive jungle, with lots of temples all through it:
Temple: x = 507, y = 70, z = 189
Temple: x = -137, y = 79, z = -459
Temple: x = -138, y = 83, z = -665
Temple: x = 261, y = 73, z = -443
Temple: x = 1177, y = 73, z = -204
Temple: x = 1350, y = 96, z = 52
Temple: x = 200, y = 75, z = 245
Temple: x = -251, y = 80, z = 180

Chapter 25
Ocean shore with extreme hills: 3145708

FROM THE AUTHOR

wanted to thank all those who are reading my books. It is heartwarming to receive all of your kind and wonderful emails through my website, www.markcheverton.com. I try to respond to all of you, but sometimes the email addresses get messed up and I cannot reply . . . I apologize for this and I'm working to get this corrected.

To those kids out there who tell me that these books are motivating you to start writing on your own, I say . . . HURRAY! Writing is a wonderful thing that can be at times exciting and terrifying. It's an easy thing to start and a really difficult thing to finish, but if you keep at it, you'll find that you can create really wonderful things. It can seem daunting at the beginning, but I've found that the best way to start writing a story is to just write . . . even if you don't know what you're doing or where your story is going. It's always easier to edit something that already exists than it is to create it. Just start writing and you'll find that the story will reveal itself to you . . . that's part of the wonderful experience. You never know what you will end up with until you actually put pen to paper or fingers to keyboard (sometimes I use both). The secret to writing is to write, and if you get stuck, then write some more . . . it can always be fixed later. Remember, you can only accomplish what you can imagine. If you want to write, then imagine yourself writing . . . and then do it. Write . . . write . . . write!

Look for *Gameknight999* and me, *Monkeypants271,* out there on the servers.

Keep reading . . . and watch out for creepers.

— Mark

AVAILABLE NOW FROM MARK CHEVERTON AND SKY PONY PRESS

THE GAMEKNIGHT999 SERIES
The world of Minecraft comes to life in this thrilling adventure!

Gameknight999 loved Minecraft, and above all else, he loved to grief—to intentionally ruin the gaming experience for other users.

But when one of his father's inventions teleports him into the game, Gameknight is forced to live out a real-life adventure inside a digital world. What will happen if he's killed? Will he respawn? Die in real life? Stuck in the game, Gameknight discovers Minecraft's best-kept secret, something not even the game's programmers realize: the creatures within the game are alive! He will have to stay one step ahead of the sharp claws of zombies and pointed fangs of spiders, but he'll also have to learn to make friends and work as a team if he has any chance of surviving the Minecraft war his arrival has started.

With deadly endermen, ghasts, and dragons, this action-packed trilogy introduces the heroic Gameknight999 and has proven to be a runaway publishing smash, showing that the Gameknight999 series is the perfect companion for Minecraft fans of all ages.

Invasion of the Overworld (Book One):
$9.99 paperback • 978-1-63220-711-1

Battle for the Nether (Book Two):
$9.99 paperback • 978-1-63220-712-8

Confronting the Dragon (Book Three):
$9.99 paperback • 978-1-63450-046-3

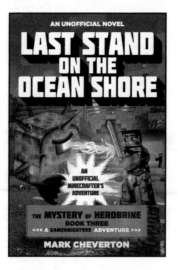

EXCERPT FROM LAST STAND ON THE OCEAN SHORE

Something's going on," Gameknight continued. "Herobrine is up to something, I can feel it. But it's too dark out there in the desert to see anything. Hunter, Stitcher: I need you two to go up to the watchtower and shoot your arrows all around the village. With the Flame enchantment on your bows, your flaming arrows will give us some light. Now GO!"

Hunter rolled her eyes at Gameknight999, then spun around quickly, her crimson locks splashing across his face. Laughing, she ran down the steps and toward the watchtower.

"Come on, Stitcher... let's light the desert up!" Hunter yelled over her shoulder as she ran.

The younger sister stepped up to Gameknight999, gave him a smile, then spun around and splashed him with her long red curls as well, laughing as she followed her older sibling.

Gameknight watched them streak to the sandstone tower. In seconds, they appeared at the top, their iridescent bows shimmering in the darkness and lighting the tower with a blue glow. Drawing back their arrows, they fired. Instantly, the tip of the arrows burst aflame with magical fire. Streaking through the darkness, the arrows looked like two tiny meteors streaking down from the heavens. When they landed, the arrows stuck deep into the pale yellow sand but continued to burn, casting a circle of light around them.

Slowly, the sisters fired more arrows out into the darkness, Hunter going to the left, and Stitcher to the right. They painted a burning arc of light along one side of the village. Gameknight stood on the wall and peered into the lit desert, looking for Herobrine and his monsters of destruction. But all he saw was brown scrub brush and green cacti, the only inhabitants in this dry wasteland.

They continued to launch their arrows into the air, the sisters competing to see who could shoot the farthest. Gradually, the two glowing arcs started to come together as Hunter and Stitcher had nearly completed the circle of flame. Gameknight peered in the dark gap that still lay hidden in shadow, the approaching flames making the shadowy area smaller and smaller. In the distance, Gameknight could just barely make out the outline of the desert temple, the spot where they'd fought the zombies.

Maybe there's a zombie-town out there somewhere?

The unlit area became smaller and smaller as Hunter and Stitcher filled in the darkness with their fiery arrows.

Did I see something move out there? Was that a flicker of gold? I must be going crazy.

Another pair of arrows streaked into the air and landed into a sand dune, casting more light into the surroundings; the circle of fire was almost complete.

Still nothing...I must be going crazy...wait...what was that?

He thought for sure he saw something out there, a dark form moving slowly through the shadows, but it had looked too big to be a monster...it had to be his imagination.

And then the sisters fired the last two arrows into the air. Gameknight watched them carve a gentle arc through the air, then landed in the ground, one of them sticking into a tall cactus, causing it to burst into flames.

But no one noticed the burning cactus.

One of the villagers screamed, then ran from the wall to find her children.

Gameknight was shocked and numb with fear.

"It can't be," Gameknight said. "No..."

"It is good to meet the User-that-is-not-a-user again," a deep voice grumbled from the desert. "This time, the outcome will be different, that can be assured."

Gameknight stared at the monster.

"How can he be here...how did he find us?" Gameknight asked, but the village was in a panic and no one heard him except for Stonecutter, who stood at his side.

"The User-that-is-not-a-user looks afraid...this is not a surprise," growled the monster.

Now, everyone could see a massive army of zombies approaching the burning circle of light, their dark claws sparkling in the fiery glow.

The monster then moved forward and stepped completely into the light of the burning arrows. Standing before them sat Xa-Tul on his massive zombie horse. The stead's eyes glowed blood red, as did the rider's. His shining chain mail sparkled in the moonlight, giving him an almost magical appearance.

Urging his mount forward another step, Xa-Tul glared up at Gameknight999, then pointed at him with his massive golden sword.

"ZOMBIES...ATTACK!" bellowed Xa-Tul, his voice making the desert itself shake with fear.

Stepping off his mount, he moved forward another step and looked straight up at Gameknight999.

"The last time, the User-that-is-not-a-user won, but this time it will be different." Xa-Tul took another step forward, then brought his sword down on a sandstone block, crushing it into dust. He then smiled and spoke in a loud gravely voice for all to hear. "Come on, user...let's dance."

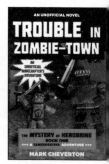

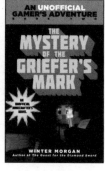
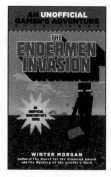

LIKE OUR BOOKS
FOR MINECRAFTERS?

Then check out other novels
by Sky Pony Press.

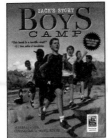

Pack of Dorks
BETH VRABEL

Boys Camp:
Zack's Story
CAMERON DOKEY,
CRAIG ORBACK

Boys Camp:
Nate's Story
KITSON JAZYNKA,
CRAIG ORBACK

Letters from an
Alien Schoolboy
R. L. ASQUITH

Just a Drop of
Water
KERRY O'MALLEY
CERRA

Future Flash
KITA HELMETAG
MURDOCK

Sky Run
ALEX SHEARER

Mr. Big
CAROL AND MATT
DEMBICKI

Available wherever books are sold!